JELLIES, JAMS, AND BODIES

JELLY SHOP MYSTERIES | BOOK 1

DONNA WALO CLANCY

Copyright © 2019 Donna Walo Clancy
Jellies, Jams, and Bodies
Jelly Shop Mysteries | Book 1
By Donna Walo Clancy

ISBN-13: 978-1798940617 [Paperback]

All characters and events in this book are a work of fiction. Any similarities to anyone living or dead are purely coincidental. Donna Walo Clancy is identified as the sole author of this book.

All rights reserved. No part of this publication maybe reproduced, stored in a retrieval system, or transmitted in any form or by any means, except for brief quotations in printed reviews, without the prior permission of the author.

Cover Design: Melissa Ringuette of Monark Design Services
Interior Formatting: Rogena Mitchell-Jones
RMJ Manuscript Service www.rogenamitchell.com

Printed in the USA
Third Edition

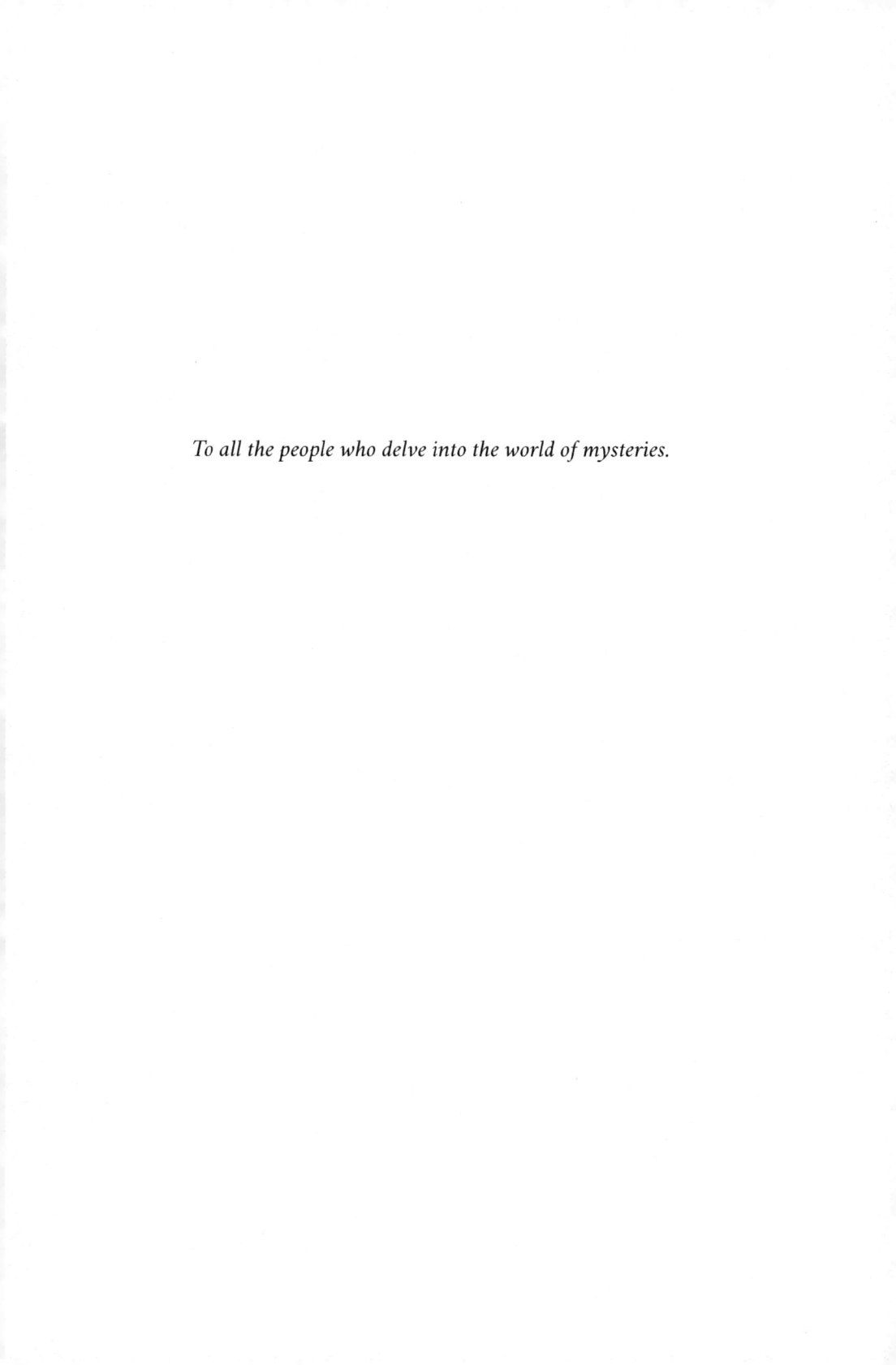

To all the people who delve into the world of mysteries.

1

The town was quiet, even for Whipper Will Junction off-season. The sun came peeking over the horizon bathed in coral and pink. The only activity in town was at the Tilted Coffee Cup. Wes Garcia and Tommy Wilbur, the owners, made sure the doors were opened, and the coffee was brewing by five-thirty every morning. Smells of fresh-baked pastries and exotic flavored coffees filled the air. Wooden two-top and four-top tables were available for those who wanted to order breakfast. Fresh flowers were placed on the tables daily. The locals filled the stools at the long silver and red counter every morning by six for coffee and gossip.

Tabby ordered two coffees to go. There was no time to waste gossiping with the locals today. They were still talking about Miss Evans being seen at the movie theater with Jamie Stokes in Larson. It was a true small-town scandal as Miss Evans was four years older than Jamie. Oh, the shame of it all! Wes tried to pull her into the conversation as he returned her change, but Tabby waved and rushed out the door. Plans had been made, and there were things to do. It was a coffee on the run kind of day.

"I think you're becoming as bad as your boyfriend," Jenny said, as Tabby walked up to the car. "Collecting 'stuff' has rubbed off on you."

"I get enough of that from my mother. Do you think I need to hear it from my best friend, too?" Tabby asked, opening the driver's side door.

Tabby and Jenny had been close since childhood. Their two totally different personalities made them perfect best friends. Jenny, five-two and a little overweight was an intellectual bookworm type who was afraid of her own shadow. Tabby, five-seven, slim and athletic, was always ready for an adventure. When a mystery presented itself, Jenny was the brains and Tabby was the brawn.

"A frog fountain? Really? We're making a three-hour trip to bid on a frog fountain?"

"It's beautiful. I want to make it the centerpiece of my new shop. The bid could have been placed by phone, but it is so nice out I thought the ride would be fun," Tabby stated, starting the car.

"It's too bad the guy opening his shop now only rented it for the busy season. You'll miss the whole summer and most of the fall tourist season, too."

"That's okay. My shop will be up and running before the Christmas holidays."

"I love the name, Jellies, Jams, and Weddings. It's kind of quirky. How in the world did you come up with a name like that?"

"I want to sell my gram's jellies in the shop. Her recipes are to die for! I also went to school to be a wedding planner. I threw everything together, and that's what I came up with."

"If you get this fountain, where are you going to keep it until your shop opens?"

"My mom said I could store it at Mystic Happenings until I can get into my building."

"Why didn't Finn come with you? He could buy more *stuff* that he doesn't need," Jenny asked, sarcastically.

"Why don't you guys like him? Mom puts him down all the time, too."

"We don't like how he uses you. He's not a bad person, just selfish," Jenny stated. "You could do so much better."

"Let's change the subject, please. I finally figured out my store budget. I can afford to bid up to two hundred dollars on the fountain."

"What is it with this fountain?"

"For some reason, when the auction catalog arrived, I felt this overwhelming need to look through it, as if something was calling out to me. The fountain is so classic! It has four levels and a lily pond at the bottom. Each level has two or three frogs in different positions that play in the cascading water. It has to be at least one hundred years old. The write-up says it was brought over from England."

"Does it work?"

"The description stated that the working condition is unknown. I can always have a new pump installed if it doesn't work."

"Do you mind if I open my window? It is so warm out for the beginning of April."

"No, go ahead. I was going to do the same thing," Tabby concurred.

They rode along the back roads toward Carson's Bend. The warm weather had already turned the desolate landscape of winter into a fresh palette of greens that is associated with the rebirth of nature in the spring.

Carson's Bend was an hour and a half away from Whipper Will Junction. It was a small town of about five hundred people. Once a month, during the good weather, the Jaspar brothers, Jim and Jerry, held auctions at their farm. They were well attended with people from as far away as Canada.

Twice a year Tabby would drive to the barn. Usually, she didn't even look at the catalog of items up for sale. But for some reason when the catalog arrived, she felt an overwhelming need to look through it. As a young girl, she had learned not to ignore the 'hunches' she sometimes got. The fountain was listed on page two. She read no further once she saw the picture of the majestic fountain. She simply had to have it for her shop.

"How's Damian doing at his new job? Does he like Scotland?" Tabby asked.

"He loves it over there. The promotion he got came with a huge raise."

"It's been three months so far, right? He'll be home before you know it."

"I don't know. He called the other night and said there was a chance they might promote him again to vice-president. That position would make the job permanent. He asked me if I would consider moving over there."

"What did you say?"

"Nothing and that's the problem. When I didn't answer him, he told me to think about it. I'm almost certain he has already taken the job."

"Don't you want to travel Europe, see the world? You've been with Damian since high school. Everyone in town figured you two would get married."

"I don't think our relationship is his top priority. He never even discussed this job opportunity with me. He showed up at the bookstore one day and said he was moving. His first concern was definitely not for me."

"I'm sorry. Do you think he would break up with you to stay there?"

"If he did, I don't think it would bother me as much as it would bother my mother," Jenny laughed.

"Seriously?" Tabby smiled.

"My mom and sister live here. I have my business, and it is doing well. In less than a year I will be able to buy the building my bookstore and apartment are in. Instead of paying rent for two spaces, I will be paying a mortgage for one building. Mr. Wells already said he would sell it to me since he wants to sell all his properties and retire to Florida."

"Maybe I can do the same thing with my building. He owns the one I am going to rent too, and the upstairs is empty. I sent him a letter asking if I could rent the upstairs as well as the store space. I'm paying almost a thousand bucks a month for my one-bedroom at the Starling Apartments."

"That's kind of pricey for the condition of those apartments," Jenny commented.

"I know. They were affordable until Fink took over the rentals. The first thing he did was raise the rent. When I got back from school it was either live there or live with my mother who can't seem to transition out of the sixties," Tabby said, rolling her eyes.

Samantha Moon, Tabby's mother, was a true hippie. Her butt length gray hair, parted in the middle, always had a beaded headband holding it in place. She wore floor-length skirts, tie-dye peasant tops, sandals year-round, and lots of jewelry. She turned her nose up at using any kind of deodorant, believing it would cause her deadly harm.

Tabby was convinced her mother had done too many drugs in her youth and time-warped herself into a permanent fogged state of mind. True to character, her mother opened a shop called Mystic Happenings when Tabby was a little girl. The business did well. Surprisingly, the unique shop had done so well that it had afforded them a comfortable life. To this day, it was still bringing in enough income for her mom to enjoy semi-retirement.

Tabby never knew who her real father was. Somewhere in the middle of peace marches, sit-ins, and the many bong parties her mother attended, she disassociated herself from the present. She stayed in the freedom of the times that were the sixties. She continued to sleep around while attending parties with others who hadn't left that time period either. Tabitha Flower Moon was born in January of nineteen ninety-one. They had moved to Whipper Will Junction when Tabby was a year old.

"Earth to Tabby. Where are you?" Jenny asked.

"Huh? What? Sorry. I was thinking about my mother," Tabby commented.

"The town hippie?" Jenny responded, smiling. "Only kidding. You know I love your mom."

"I know you do, just like I love your mom."

"So, why are you so deep in thought?"

"It's funny, I swore to myself when I left for school I would never return here. My mom has always been the joke of the town. People still laugh at her behind her back after years of living here. They like her and respect her, but they still snicker. She has stayed here all this time. Your mom is the only one who never laughed at her."

"My mom loves her like a sister. They spent so much time together as we grew up it was natural that we would become best friends. What brought all this up?"

"I was thinking. They have never left here. You have a chance to go see Europe, but you would rather stay. I came back after school. What is it about this town?"

"It's not the town. It's the people in the town. Plus, what we don't have available here, Larsen has twenty minutes away."

"The people are nice. A little quick to judge, but nice," Tabby agreed. "The tourist season does keep the town lively."

"I think your business will take off, Tabs. Whipper Will Junction is the perfect destination spot. It has beautiful Fuller's Point with two different beaches during the summer, and the surrounding mountains dressed in their fall colors would make the perfect backdrop for an autumn wedding."

"That's true. I have to start making connections so that I can put my bridal packages together. There is so much to do before the store actually opens. I should make you my PR person."

"Thanks, but no thanks. I have enough of my own work to do at the book store. Maybe you could show off your planning skills with your own wedding. It's about time Finn stepped up and made a commitment."

"I don't see that happening any time soon." Tabby laughed.

"Yeah, I believe that," Jenny mumbled.

"Don't start."

"Exit thirty-two, one mile," Jenny announced. "We're almost there."

"I figured we'd get here early so we could check out the other auction items. I want to look over the fountain before the bidding starts."

"I hope there are some old books I can bid on for the bookstore."

Tabby slowed down for the exit. At the end of the ramp, she took a left.

"There's a coffee shop up ahead. Do you want another coffee or something to eat?"

"How long do you think the auction will take?"

"It starts at nine. We should be out between eleven and one, depending on when the fountain comes up for sale," Tabby replied.

"We should get a muffin or something. That will hold us over until we can get lunch on the way home."

They pulled in to the local shop which was already buzzing with activity. Customers were enjoying breakfast while looking over the auction catalog. Many of them were placing check marks on the items they wanted to bid on.

"This is going to be a big auction since it is the first one of the season. I hope no one wants the fountain," Tabby whispered. "I left my catalog at home. Would you grab one off the counter for me?"

Fresh coffee and toasted blueberry muffins in hand, the girls climbed in the car to head to Jaspar's Barn. Big signs posted on the side of the road alerted them that Jaspar's was coming up on the right. A large field served as the parking lot for the auction house. It was already over half full.

The Jaspar Farm was a working farm until ten years ago. Now the only section of the farm harvested were the apple trees in the fall. The brothers lived in an updated farmhouse at the rear of the property.

The large grain silo had windows cut out of the metal walls, electricity added, and large ceiling fans installed to cool down the inside in the summer. It was attached to a rundown barn where the actual auctions took place.

People were milling about waiting for the viewing room doors to open. Some were peering into the windows trying to get a glimpse of what was going on inside. Many were flipping through the pages of the auction catalog. Jenny was looking for the books.

"There are eight lots of books up for auction," Jenny stated. "Three of the lots have old books that would look awesome in the front window of my bookstore."

"Are you going to bid on them?"

"I brought the store charge card just in case I saw something worth spending my money on," Jenny answered.

The silo doors slid open, and the rush was on.

"Come on, let's hurry in and find a good seat."

The grain silo was lined with make-shift tables of saw horses and old doors. Hundreds of items were displayed on the wooden door-tops for viewing. A small tent of cardboard with the corresponding number to the listing in the catalog was placed in front of each item.

"We have an hour to walk around. First, I am going to find the fountain. It must be at the back of the room where all the bigger pieces are. Do you want to come see it with me?"

"Sure, I can look at the books later. I have to see this fountain that can 'call' to people," Jenny laughed. "Lead the way."

They meandered to the back of the room. Bureaus, desks, beds, and other furniture were set up for people to inspect. The girls made their way through the space checking everywhere, but they couldn't find the fountain. Finally, Tabby asked one of the Jaspar brothers where it was located.

"The fountains are out in back of the barn. You go through those doors over there," he said, pointing to the far corner of the silo. "There are six of them. Which one are you interested in?"

"I love the frog fountain," Tabby responded.

"That one's a big draw today. I know of at least four people here just for that item, plus we have three phone bidders registered that couldn't be here. Good luck getting that one," Jerry said, shaking his head.

"Looks like your fountain called out to a lot of people, not just you," Jenny observed.

"Come on," Tabby said, heading for the doors that led out back.

Once outside, they found the fountains set up to the right side of the barn. Several people were strolling around, stopping at each fountain to look it over. Tabby stopped abruptly as she saw a large crowd peering at what she already thought of as HER fountain.

"This just stinks," she said, frowning.

"Think positive," Jenny suggested. "Maybe you have a bigger budget than they do."

"All this way for nothing..." Tabby mumbled.

"I tell you what, if you need to, you are welcome to use my charge card to get the fountain. I didn't realize just how much you really wanted those old frogs. Set your new budget at four hundred, okay?"

Tabby grabbed her best friend and gave her a huge hug.

"I have two hundred cash with me. If I need your card, I'll give you the cash right away and pay you the rest when we get home. You're the best."

"All right, already. Let go of me. Let's go look at this frog thing," Jenny said, smiling brightly.

The friends waited for some of the viewers to walk away. Tabby walked around to the back. The fountain was approximately eight feet tall and five feet wide. The lily pond at the bottom was a little bit wider than the rest of the fountain. There were eight frogs in different positions on the four levels. They were placed in such a way that the cascading water would splash around them, making it look like they were playing in the stream. Jenny shuffled noisily to the back of the unusual fountain to join Tabby in her perusal.

"Does it look like it works?" Jenny questioned.

"Truthfully, it looks like the whole inner workings need to be gutted and replaced."

"How much will that cost?"

"At least two to three hundred, I'm afraid."

"Is it still worth it?"

"To me it is. I have totally fallen in love with this fountain. It's even more beautiful in person. Don't you wonder where it came from and who else has owned it over the last one hundred years?"

"My brain doesn't think like yours. I don't see a mystery in everything I look at."

"Do I really do that?"

"Yes, you do. Let's go check the books so I know what I want to bid on. Then we'll register, get our paddle numbers, and grab seats as close to the front as we can."

They found the book table and Jenny went through the different lots to see if she wanted to bid on any of them. She decided on two lots that had both old and new books. They registered, and each got their own number to bid with. The closest seats they could get to the front was in row eight. They sat and waited for the auction to begin.

"We still have ten minutes. Can you save the seats while I go find a bathroom?" Jenny requested. "All that coffee is catching up with me."

"Sure, go ahead. I'll be right here."

Tabby looked around and saw that all the chairs were filling up fast. To the right of the room was a row of desks where the registered phone bidders could call. A person was stationed at each one ready to operate their phone and yell out their caller's bid. Jenny returned to her seat just as the auctioneer walked up to the podium.

"Did I miss anything?"

"No, it's just starting," Tabby whispered.

The first hour passed with jewelry, paintings, and vases being sold and then the books came up for auction. Jenny bid on both lots that she wanted, and to her surprise, won each of them for a reasonable price.

"Let's hope I'm as lucky as you in my bidding," Tabby said, smiling.

The auctioneer announced a half an hour break. The girls left their paddles on their chairs and got up to stretch. They walked out to the silo to see what was left to bid on.

"It looks like it's just the big pieces left. That means the fountains should be coming up soon. I'm going to run to the bathroom. I'll meet you back at the seats," Tabby stated.

The auctioneer returned to the podium. Jerry Jaspar was setting up photos of the fountains that were outside.

"We are moving forward to the fountain lots. Phone attendants, please get our three registered phone bidders on the line."

Three of the fountains were auctioned off for between fifty and two hundred dollars each. Jerry placed the picture of the frog fountain on the easel.

"Phone attendants, do we have our three bidders on the line?"

"Here we go!" Tabby exclaimed, sitting straight up in her chair so her paddle would be seen easily.

"Are the phone bidders ready?"

The attendants nodded their heads.

"Let's begin the bidding at fifty dollars."

Tabby's paddle shot up.

"We have fifty, do I hear seventy-five?"

Another paddle shot up.

"I have seventy-five, looking for one hundred."

"Two hundred," yelled one of the phone attendants.

"I have two hundred. Do I hear two-twenty-five?"

Tabby raised her paddle again.

Jellies, Jams, and Bodies

"I have two-twenty-five. Do I hear two-fifty?"

"Three hundred," hollered the same phone attendant again.

"Darn," Tabby muttered.

"Three hundred, do I hear three-fifty?"

Tabby raised her paddle.

"I have three-fifty. Do I hear four hundred?"

Tabby held her breath. One more bid and she was out.

"Four twenty-five," countered the phone attendant one more time.

"Keep bidding," Jenny encouraged.

"I can't," Tabby confided sadly.

"I have four twenty-five. Do I hear four-fifty?"

Tabby didn't move. Jenny grabbed her paddle and waved it in the air.

"We have four-fifty. Do I hear four-seventy-five?"

"What are you doing?" Tabby demanded.

"We had to try one more time," Jenny offered.

"Five hundred," bellowed the same phone representative.

Tabby grabbed the paddle from her best friend's hand and sat on it. She knew Jenny would keep bidding just to get the fountain for her no matter what the cost.

"No more," Tabby whispered. "We tried."

"I have five hundred. Do I hear five twenty-five?"

Silence. No paddles were raised in the air.

"I have five hundred once, five hundred twice, five hundred three times, and sold for five hundred dollars to the phone bidder at station two."

The girls got up to leave.

"Well, at least you got some books for your store. It wasn't a total waste of time," Tabby stated, trying to smile. "Let's pick up your books and go get some lunch."

On the way home the girls stopped at a small café just outside of town and enjoyed a nice lunch on the patio under the bright sunshine. They could have driven another twenty minutes and eaten in Whipper Will Junction, but it was nice to eat without the local drama and gossip.

They drove to the Tilted Coffee Cup to pick up Jenny's car from the parking lot since she had to drive right back to the book store. Her assistant, Sienna, had worked by herself all morning so Jenny could go to the auction. They transferred the four boxes of books to Jenny's back seat, and with a wave, she was off to work.

Tabby had to tell her mom she didn't win the bid. Samantha had been cleaning a spot in the back room of Mystic Happenings to store the fountain for her daughter.

It was such a nice day she decided to walk to her mom's store at the other end of town. Everyone she passed was smiling and in a good mood. Several of the storefronts on Main Street were showing signs of life. Many of the smaller businesses closed for the winter and re-opened in the early spring for the beginning of tourist season.

Tabby stopped in front of the store site she would be renting in the fall and peered through the window. There were boxes piled everywhere, and a new counter had been installed at the far end of the room. Sam Pierce, the man that was opening the Baseball Card Shop, was nowhere to be seen. Tabby wanted to check with him to see if he was using the upstairs space for storage. The shop had a large cellar that was plenty big enough for stock. She wanted to rent the upstairs apartment and move out of the place she was in now.

2

"I wish I had known you wanted this space right away," a voice said from behind her. "I never would have rented it to Mr. Pierce for just the summer season."

"Oh, Mr. Wells, you startled me," Tabby answered, turning around.

"I would rather have rented this building to a local than to an outsider. I tried to rent Mr. Pierce the larger shop at the end of town. I even offered the other place for the same price as this one. He insisted on renting this shop instead."

"I was looking for Mr. Pierce, then I was coming to see you," Tabby responded, giving the elderly man a hug.

"Does this mean I am finally getting the date I want with you?" he asked, winking.

"Mr. Wells, you're incorrigible. I sent you a letter about the possibility of renting the upstairs apartment here."

"I suppose that could be arranged," Mr. Wells replied.

"Jenny told me you are selling her the bookstore building. She is so excited. I was hoping maybe we could come up with the same kind of deal for this building."

"I would love to see my buildings go to locals. The Starling Apartments are already up for sale. Some big-time developer wants to buy them just to tear them down. I can't do that to the people living there."

"I am so glad you are not going to sell to them," Tabby responded.

"Since these old bones can't take the winters here anymore, Florida is calling my name. I can take my time selling the rental houses because they will still provide income even if I leave. Some of my places have to be sold right away so I have the money to move and buy a new place down south."

"Who is selling everything for you?" Tabby inquired. "Larry Fink?"

"No, I don't like him. I think he is a snake," Mr. Wells groused, shaking his head. "I wish I had looked into his background a little more before I signed an agreement with him and handed all my rentals over to him."

"Join the club. A lot of people around here don't trust him. He's so creepy," Tabby replied, shivering. "Did you know he raised all the rents at the Starling Apartments?"

"He what?" Mr. Wells demanded, his voice rising with his anger.

"About six months ago. You didn't know?" Tabby inquired.

"No, I didn't. That will be taken care of immediately. He thinks I am just an old man who is losing his mind and doesn't know what's going on. I knew he was a snake. That's why I'm going to Larsen to hire a Miss Carver from Rose Point Realty as my sales agent. She's new to the office, but they say she's a spitfire and gets the job done. Looks like she will be taking care of my rentals from now on, too."

"I think that will be a smart thing to do," Tabby encouraged him. "Do I have to talk to Larry Fink about renting upstairs or should I wait until you change things over to Miss Carver?"

"Neither, I still have the final say over what happens to my properties. When do you want to move in?" he asked.

"Really? How about now?" Tabby responded with her warmest smile.

"Now?"

"Only kidding. How about the first of May? I know Sierra Holt has been waiting for a place to open up at Starling. She could have the apartment I am in, and you wouldn't lose any rent. In fact, you'd be gaining rent because the space above the store has been empty for a while now."

"Smart girl. Are you this good at talking your way into everything you want, or am I just an old softie?" Mr. Wells laughed.

"You're just an old softie, but I won't tell anyone, don't worry," Tabby whispered, batting her eyes at the old man.

"Oh, I have a little something for you. I saw this the other day and knew you had to have it for your new shop."

He extended his hand and lying in it was a small teddy bear that was light brown, six inches tall, and holding a small jar of strawberry jelly in its little paws.

"That is so cute. He will sit on the register to greet everyone," Tabby smiled, taking the bear.

"I'm going to see Fink now. You will need keys to move your things in over the next couple of weeks. I will make sure Fink gets them to you as quick as possible. You don't have to pay rent until the first. How does four hundred a month sound? No charge for move-in time."

"You are so awesome," Tabby replied, grabbing the old man in a big bear hug.

"If I knew this was all it took to get so many hugs, I would have suggested it a long time ago," Mr. Wells said, his eyes twinkling. "I'll be in touch."

Tabby watched her elderly friend walk away. He was one of the people who had influenced her decision to move back to Whipper Will Junction. Growing up, he had been like the grandfather that Tabby never had. All the townspeople loved Mr. Wells. He owned most of the buildings, but he had made a point to keep the rents low so that his tenants didn't have to struggle to maintain a decent life. Mr. Wells was one of those people that gave back more than he had ever received.

Tabby took one last look through the window of the store. In the reflection, she saw Fink staring from across the street.

I wonder how long he's been watching us.

She turned around to look at Fink, and he scurried inside the door to his realty company.

Soon this space would be her new gift shop—Jellies, Jams, and

Weddings. It would open October first if all went well. Halloween would be her first real holiday in the new store, and she was excited because it was also her favorite holiday! She couldn't wait to decorate the big picture window so people passing by would stop and look and hopefully come inside to shop.

She continued strolling down Main Street. Mac was sweeping the sidewalk in front of his store. James MacAvey owned the only market in town, and he always kept it well stocked. If you couldn't find what you needed at Mac's Market, then you really didn't need it.

"Good morning, Tabby," he smiled, leaning on his broom.

"Hello to you, Mr. MacAvey."

"How many times do I have to tell you to call me James?"

"I keep forgetting. When you grow up calling a person one thing, it's hard to change."

"I guess. Will you be in the cable office on Monday? I'm having trouble with my bill again. This is the second month in a row they've screwed it up."

"I'll be there. Bring it in, and I'll figure it out," Tabby answered. "Got to run. I'm on my way to see my mom."

"Say hi to her for me."

"I will. See you soon."

She arrived at her mother's shop with no more interruptions. Samantha was in the front window, setting up a new display of colorful crystals. The afternoon sun was shining on the beautiful display creating rainbows which were complemented by the lilac satin material underneath. Her mother definitely knew how to create an eye-catching display. The beauty of the window would draw people into the shop.

Tabby waltzed into the shop as her mom crawled out of the window space.

"The window looks beautiful," Tabby complimented, hugging her mom. "I'm going to have real competition for the best window on Main Street when my store opens."

"I've been doing this a lot of years," her mom said, walking over to the register counter. "You'll have to do your best to beat me in the holiday window contests."

"It looks like I have to come up with a different store plan for my shop. I didn't win the frog fountain," Tabby remarked, picking up an amethyst necklace.

"Oh honey, I'm sorry. I know how badly you wanted that fountain. What did it go for?"

"One of the phone bidders got it for five hundred dollars."

"Darn, for an old frog fountain? That's crazy."

"I know, but it was so beautiful. When I finally saw it in person, I wanted it even more," Tabby answered sadly.

"You'll come up with something else," her mom responded, sorting the remaining crystals in the box. "Have you checked out the new flower shop at the end of town? It's far out."

"No, not yet. I need to go there and set up an account for the shop. I'll see if their wedding flowers are up to par with my arrangements and bouquets."

"I love your arrangements, they are so unique. I have always said you should have opened a flower shop, and now someone has beat you to it. Do you like these?" she asked, holding up several strands of Love Beads.

"They're nice. My shop will showcase my flower arrangements in the wedding packages. I'm still trying to tighten my merchandise line for the brides. The tourists will love Gram's jams and jellies. I am going to sell the jars individually as well as use them in gift baskets."

"You should sell Gram's biscuits to go with the jellies. I have her recipe around here somewhere," her mother offered as she crawled back into the small window space again.

"That's a great idea. They always smelled so good when she was baking them. I talked to Mr. Wells about renting the upstairs apartment above the shop so I can do all my cooking there. If I leave the windows open while I make the jams, jellies, and biscuits, the smell should reach all the way up and down Main Street. That will pull in paying customers."

"I'm glad you are getting out of those apartments. It will be nice to have you in town."

"I told Mr. Wells about the rent increase. He was absolutely furious.

Mr. Fink raised the rents without telling him. He was going over to the real estate office and have it out with the sneaky jerk."

"I am so glad I bought my building from Richard ten years ago. It's almost paid off. I have one year left, and it will be all mine. I wish it had an upstairs apartment like your building does. Maybe once I own it, I can add on a second floor. Right now, I'm happy living with Jill and Judy at the bed and breakfast. Something to think about for the future, I guess."

"I'm going to run. I want to see if Mr. Pierce is at his shop yet so I can get upstairs and see how big it is and what kind of shape it is in. I'll talk to you tomorrow. Love you," Tabby said, hugging her mom.

"Don't forget you promised to help with the Summer Kick-Off Weekend. We have our first meeting tomorrow night at the library at six-thirty. Will you be there?"

"Yes. I'll make supper early so I can be there on time."

"Why don't you just meet us at the diner? We all go there to eat before the first meeting every year."

"I have to cook supper for Finn," Tabby answered, realizing too late that she shouldn't have said that.

"Can't that loser cook for himself?"

"He's not a loser, Mom."

"He is a loser and a user. He's probably at your place right now, asleep, waiting for you to come home and make supper. My cat treats me better than he treats you. There's a lot more fish out in the sea, you know."

"You and Jen have been spending way too much time together. You sound just alike. I'll see you at the meeting tomorrow night," she said, shaking her head as she walked out the door.

The closer Tabby got to the center of town, the louder the yelling became. Everyone walking on Main Street had stopped in front of her future shop and was listening to the argument that was taking place inside the real estate office across the street. The windows were open, and the locals could hear every word being said.

Tabby looked around. This had to be a new record. A crowd was gathering, and Gladys Twittle was nowhere to be found. Donald Twittle and his wife owned the Penny Poor Antique Shop two doors up from Tabby's building. If there ever were two people that fit the 'opposites attract' theory, it was Donald and Gladys. He was a quiet, pleasant man, and well-liked in the town.

His wife was as wide as she was tall. The locals never knew what color Gladys would dye her hair for the coming week as she always tried to match the bright colors in the flower print dresses that she loved to wear.

Known as 'The Town Mouth,' she had a way of showing up at the right place at the right time. She never missed anything. The next morning you would find her on the first stool at the Tilted Coffee Cup, next to the register, telling everyone the latest gossip. She knew everything, and if she didn't, she would dig until she did. She was pushy and bossy and not liked at all.

True to her nature, Gladys came waddling up the street. She stopped at the edge of the crowd, next to Mrs. Ryan, the second nosiest person in town.

"What have I missed already?" Gladys asked in a loud voice.

"Shhh," Mrs. Ryan urged as the voices started up again from across the street.

Where have you been?

I was out taking care of some business.

What business? Anything to do with my holdings?

Just business.

Who told you that it was acceptable to raise all the rents on my properties? You didn't discuss it with me.

I'm doing my job, trying to make you more money.

I have plenty of money. I believe you raised the rents to raise your commission fees, that's what I think.

You have no idea how this business really works. You're just an old man who is set in his old ways. If you really knew what was going on in your buildings, you would have a heart attack.

Well, this old man is pulling all my business from your office as of right now. I will be back at four o'clock this afternoon for all my files, keys, and anything else that pertains to my properties. I will be returning with the sheriff because I don't trust you. Have everything ready for me including a final bill of commissions owed to you up to today's date.

You can't do this to me. You own seventy percent of everything in town. Without your business, I have nothing.

Fink glanced out the window, and to his mortification, he realized they had an audience. He slammed the window closed, shutting out any noise that could escape out to the listening crowd. Several minutes later, Mr. Wells stormed out the front door. His face was red which made his snow-white hair stand out even more than usual. The veins were bulging in his neck. He walked straight to the sheriff's office at the edge of the town green.

"That was interesting," Tabby commented, breaking the silence of the crowd.

People nodded in agreement. The show being over, the locals continued on their way. Mrs. Ryan followed Mrs. Twittle into her shop where they would no doubt analyze everything they just heard and come up with their own conclusions. Tabby noticed that Mr. Pierce had been standing in the door of the shop listening to everything being said. He seemed very interested in what was going on even though he had moved to town only a month ago.

"Mr. Pierce, may I speak with you a moment?" Tabby requested, moving toward the shop door.

"And you are?" he asked.

"My name is Tabitha Moon. I am renting this shop space when you leave in September."

"Yes, I recall Mr. Wells mentioning that to me. What can I do for you?"

"I am moving into the apartment above the shop next week. I was hoping you would let me upstairs so I can see what needs to be done before I move in," Tabby replied. "I live a quiet lifestyle. It will be myself and my boyfriend most nights."

"Mr. Fink didn't say anything about anyone renting upstairs. I have stock up there. If you hold on for a minute, I'll go up and close the boxes and then you can look around."

"That's fine. I have all afternoon."

Jellies, Jams, and Bodies

Sam Pierce disappeared up the inside stairway that connected the shop space to the apartment above. Tabby walked around checking out her future rental space. It was a good size. There was a small back room that she could use as a workspace. The stairs to the basement were located to the right of the small bathroom in the back corner of the shop. Maybe she could talk Mr. Pierce into selling her the new counter when he left. It would be perfect for her register area.

"Everything's set. You can go up and look around. I will move the boxes down to the basement over the weekend. It's pretty dirty up there. I don't think anyone has used the apartment for a long time."

"I think the last person to live up there was Mrs. Ryan. Her husband died, and she didn't want to live so far out of town, so she sold their house and moved into the apartment here. That was like… eight years ago. She lives at the bed and breakfast now because the stairs got to be too much for her to climb every day. Thank you for making time for me. I'll be down shortly."

Tabby climbed up the back stairs not knowing what to expect. Mr. Pierce was right. It was filthy. It would take a week of cleaning every day just to bring it up to a livable condition. The living room was a good size and at the front of the building overlooking the street. The kitchen was small but had everything she needed. The bathroom only had a stand-up shower and no tub. A large bedroom with a big walk-in closet was at the back.

There was a smaller room that could be used as a second bedroom or a storage area. Tabby decided she would use this area to store her jellies and any inventory that she would acquire over the summer. The whole place could definitely use a fresh coat of paint.

In the far corner, she noticed something had been covered with a blanket. She walked over and peeked underneath. A telescope perched on a tripod had been hidden from view.

As she continued to look around, she noticed three small circle impressions in the dust on the floor, directly in front of the bay window. The telescope must have been moved from that spot and hidden under the blanket so Tabby wouldn't know what he was up to.

Mr. Pierce had just rented the space, yet he was watching someone or something.

Who or what is he watching?

She stood inside the triangular area that the three circles formed on the floor to see where the telescope was focused. The only place in the direct line of vision was Whipper Will Real Estate. Tabby noticed several black boxes piled behind the telescope that had wires hanging out the sides. On top of one of the boxes was a set of headphones. As she stood looking out the window, Mr. Pierce appeared in the doorway.

"Are you almost done? I have someplace I have to be," he inquired, staring at the covered telescope.

Tabby didn't want him to know she had been nosy and snooped under the blanket.

"I was looking out the window and thinking what a beautiful view I will have of the town green when the fall colors appear. That's my favorite time of year, the fall. What's your favorite time of year, Mr. Pierce?" she asked, continuing to look out the window.

"Uh, I don't know. I never really thought about it. Look, I really must get going. Are you done?" the antsy Mr. Pierce asked again.

"Yes, I am. I will see you on Monday. Thank you for your time," Tabby responded, as she gave him her best smile and hurried past him.

3

On the drive home, she was deep in thought trying to figure out what Mr. Pierce was doing with his telescope. It couldn't be the stars. The buildings and trees on Main Street blocked any kind of view of the sky. Maybe he was a pervert and was looking in people's windows. All the buildings on the opposite side of the street had apartments on the second floor. She would have to do more nosing around on Monday.

Finn's truck was already in the parking lot when she arrived at home. She strolled into her apartment, threw her keys on the table, and stepped over to the fridge to reach in for a refreshing wine cooler. Her boyfriend was asleep in the recliner just like her mother said he would be. He didn't work this time of year so why was he always so tired? It was Saturday night which meant beans and hotdogs for supper. Why couldn't they go out for dinner? Some things never changed.

Tabby sipped her drink, looking at Finn. She wanted things to change. She needed things to change. Finn Morton had been her boyfriend since the first summer she came home from college. They met at the local drive-in where she worked a summer job to earn money for school. They had been dating for six years. It was a weird relationship. He was there every night for supper, but the word 'commitment' was apparently not in his vocabulary or his plans. He wanted to come and go as he pleased and do what he wanted when he wanted. Why hadn't she acknowledged this before now? Why did she continue to deny what had been in front of her face for a very long time? Her stomach churned as her emotions boiled.

It had been over a year since he had taken her out on a date or spent any money on her. He was at her apartment every night to eat supper but never brought any food with him. People around town said he was a user, a self-centered cheapskate. The top priority in his life were his *things*, and he was a collector of everything. Sometimes, Tabby felt like his stuff was more important than she was. So why did she always step up and defend him? Maybe she was afraid to move on. It had been so long since she dated and tried different things. Tabby was obviously stuck in a very deep rut. But did she really want to stay there?

Every day it was work and come home to be at Finn's beck and call. Her mom's and best friend's words were starting to ring true. He was gorgeous to look at, but that was about it. Is this what her life was going to be like forever? The longer she watched him sleep, the more furious she became. She did deserve better. A lot better.

Finn woke up and looked over to see Tabby staring at him.

"Like what you see?" he asked, smiling confidently.

"Not so much," she answered, walking into the bathroom and closing the door with a slam.

While sitting in the bathroom, Tabby weighed the pros and cons of her relationship with Finn. The more upset she became, the more her stomach lurched, and she almost threw up. It had to end tonight, or she wouldn't have the gumption to do it again for a while. She would let things slide and look the other way as she always did.

She came out of the bathroom fifteen minutes later hoping that he had left, but no such luck. He was in the kitchen making his nightly drink. Tabby didn't feel like dealing with this tonight, but she knew she had to. Her mood was not going to improve. Maybe she was depressed because of not winning the fountain, and everything was making her mad. No, she was sure it was Finn and his ways that had finally got to her.

She went to the living room, turned on the news, and guzzled her wine cooler, wishing she had picked up a second one out of the fridge before she sat down. Then she saw it—a pile of stuff tossed in the corner of her living room.

"What is that?" she asked, pointing to the corner.

"What is what?" he responded, looking at where she was pointing.

"That."

"I bought that stuff at the flea market today. I didn't have any room at my place for it, so I brought it over here," he answered, sitting down on the couch next to her.

"No! My place is not going to become a storage unit like your place. Get it out of here now!"

"Where am I going to put it?"

"I really don't care. Put it in your truck or anywhere, but not here," she demanded, crossing her arms. "Tonight. I want it out of here tonight."

"What set you off?"

"I don't want to talk about it right now," she replied, continuing to stare at the television. "I'd really like to be by myself tonight. Take your stuff and go."

"No supper?"

"Go eat at the diner."

"Fine, but I'm taking my drink with me," he said. "I don't know what your problem is."

"You want to know what my problem is? You are my problem. You bring all your crap over here without asking, you eat over here every night without ever contributing anything to the meals, and you haven't taken me out on a date or spent a cent on me in over a year. Most people that have been together for six years are engaged or married."

"You know how I feel about marriage."

"I sure do. You want a place to crash unless you have made other plans, supper cooked for you every night, and no commitment. Well, you know what? No more. I'm done. Take your stuff and get out. I'm breaking up with you."

"Are you serious?"

"Yes, I am. Dead serious. Don't take the drink with you, it's my glass," Tabby demanded, storming over to the fridge and opening a second wine cooler.

Finn downed the drink and then threw the glass at the kitchen sink, shattering the glass everywhere.

"There's your glass," he yelled.

Finn picked up as much as he could carry from the pile that sat in the corner. He brushed past her with the first load. She watched him out the window as he flung everything into the back of his truck. He marched into the kitchen and picked up the bottle of gin.

"This is mine. I paid for it," he declared, staring her down, waiting for her to disagree.

"Whatever," Tabby responded. "Just get the rest of your stuff and go."

"Nobody ditches Finn Morten. You'll be sorry," he added in a threatening voice as he stalked out the door. "You'll be calling me."

"I doubt it," she yelled, closing the door with a slam and locking it.

She watched him get in the truck and speed away. The tears came suddenly out of nowhere- what had she just done? Six years down the drain. Six wasted years. She opened and guzzled a third wine cooler, then grabbed the fourth and last one and threw herself on the couch to drink it at a slower pace.

In between the tears, a feeling of relief washed over her. Tabby could get past this. It would hurt tonight, but tomorrow things would look better. She had a new place to live, a new business starting soon, and now, a new and better love life to find.

She must have been listening subconsciously to her mother and Jen all this time. The pile of stuff in the living room had been the final straw. Just wait until Jen heard that now they would be single together at the same time. This might not be so bad. In fact, it might actually be fun.

Tomorrow night Tabby would show up for supper before the meeting. She would tell her mother about the break-up and watch her dance around the diner. For the next week, she would be the number one story in all the local gossip. Losing the fountain, the break-up, and now the flood of tears had taken its toll on her. She crawled into bed, exhausted.

Tabby didn't wake up until ten thirty the next morning. She had slept right through church. Luckily, she hadn't been on greeting or refreshment duty. Spending the day in pajamas wasn't such a bad idea. It had been a long time since she took a day for herself. She made a nice breakfast of blueberry pancakes and bacon with fresh squeezed orange juice. Finn always wanted eggs and sausage. He wouldn't even try her world-famous pancakes. From now on, she could have whatever she wanted for breakfast. The more she thought about it, the more she liked the idea of being single.

Her cell phone rang. She could hear it buzzing but couldn't find it. Where did she leave it last night? It stopped ringing before she could get to it. She didn't want to answer it anyway. This was her liberation day, and she was darn well going to enjoy it. Anyone trying to call her would think that she was with Finn and that was why she didn't answer. Boy, were they going to be surprised.

Tabby stayed on the couch most of the day reading a mystery novel. She loved a good mystery and had read every one the library carried. Her common sense and analytical mind made it easy for her to figure out who the killer was before the end of the book or movie. She had never been able to put her deducing talent to work in real life as nothing exciting ever happened in the small town of Whipper Will Junction.

She made a list of things she would need to buy to get her new apartment in livable condition. The list contained mostly cleaners. She would work during the day at the cable company and go clean for a few hours each night until the weekend when she would be able to finish the cleaning. If she rented a small moving truck, she could move everything the following weekend. Now that Finn wasn't around, she had to find someone to help her move. Maybe she could pay some of the high school seniors to assist her. She'd have to check around.

When her cell phone went off again, she looked at the screen and saw it was Finn calling, so she didn't answer. It was over, and he was going to have to accept that. Nothing he could say would bring them back together. She threw the phone on the couch and headed for the shower. The committee members were meeting at the diner at five o'clock. Her day of leisure was over. It was time to get back to the real world.

At five-fifteen, Tabby pulled into the diner parking lot. Her mother's car was already there along with several other cars she recognized as belonging to committee members. She entered the diner and strolled to the back room that was used primarily for private functions.

"Well look who's here," Tom Montgomery said, smiling. "Glad you could make it."

"I thought you were making supper for Finn tonight," her mom piped up sarcastically.

"About that. I broke up with Finn last night. We're done," Tabby casually stated, waiting for the emotional geyser that was about to take place.

"Excuse me? Did I hear that right?" her mother squealed, leaping to her feet.

"You heard me right."

Samantha Moon let out a shriek. She danced around waving her skirt and hugging and kissing everyone that was seated at the table. Tommy Wilbur let out a "thank goodness." There were several other hallelujahs and hand-clapping from the committee members. Tabby had expected a scene from her mother, but not from the rest of the town.

The patrons in the diner were watching what was happening in the function room. There was much whispering and smiling. Donald and Gladys sat in the booth closest to the back room. Tabby was sure she asked to be placed there to spy on the committee supper. Now she had some real gossip to give to the early morning coffee drinkers at the Tilted Coffee Cup.

"Does Jen have any idea?" her mom asked gleefully.

"No, not yet. I was going to tell her on the way to work when I stop with her morning coffee," Tabby commented. "Can we just drop this for now?"

"Sure, I'm sorry. I didn't mean to make a public spectacle of you. I'm sure Gladys got an earful. Unfortunately, you'll be the talk of the town for the next few days. You have absolutely no idea how happy you have made me tonight!" she said, giving Tabby a hug as she sat down next to her.

"Drinks are on me," Samantha announced. "The first round, anyway."

The fourteen-member committee had a great time while eating. They laughed, reminisced about the past Summer Kick-Off Weekends, and discussed who else they could finagle into working on the celebration.

"Why don't we assign committee heads and call it a night," Tommy suggested. "We have another meeting next Sunday night at the library. We can get down to business then."

Assignments were handed out without too much complaining. Tabby and Jen were assigned to head the Blue-Ribbon Contests. They would be responsible for organizing all entries in cooking, quilting, and the What I Am Doing This Summer short stories submitted by the local school-age children. Tabby loved to read the compositions entered by the kids. They had such vivid imaginations.

It was eight o'clock when the meeting ended. The rest of the diner had already emptied. Once outside, Tabby's mother gave her another long hug.

"You will never know how happy you made me tonight. I know as your mother I am supposed to support you in everything you do, but I just couldn't with that loser you called a boyfriend. What made you change your mind?"

"He brought a pile of stuff over to my house and plopped it in my living room. He didn't ask if he could, he just did it. That was the final straw. He can have a nice life with his things. I hope they keep him warm at night," Tabby replied. "You and Jen were right. I guess most of the town was right."

"It wasn't a matter of being right. It was a matter of what was best for you" her mother said, kissing the top of her head. "We all love you."

"I know. It doesn't hurt as bad as I thought it would. I'll be fine."

"Love you much. Please be careful going home," her mother instructed, climbing into her own car.

Tabby slid into the front seat and began the short drive home.

When she arrived, she found her front door standing ajar which caused the hairs on the back of her neck to stand up. She knew that she had locked the apartment up tight when she left.

Tabby took her pepper spray out of her purse. Her hand slid in between the door and the frame to the light switch. The overhead light came on in the living room. There was no noise in the apartment. She pushed the door open and stepped in.

To her horror, the place had been destroyed. Furniture was sliced and ripped open, and every shelf had been emptied of its contents and dumped onto the floor. She took out her cell phone and dialed 911. The dispatcher put her through to Sheriff Puckett, and he promised to get there as fast as he could. He instructed her to go back to her car and lock herself in until he arrived.

Two cruisers flew into the parking lot with lights flashing and sirens screaming. People were coming out of the other apartments to see what was going on. Tabby exited her car and walked over to the sheriff.

"What happened, Tabby?" Sheriff Puckett questioned.

"Someone destroyed my place," she answered with a shiver. "I found the front door open when I got home."

"Stay here while we go check it out."

Tabby watched the officers disappear inside. The lights went on in each room as they crept through looking for a suspect. The sheriff exited the apartment and called her over.

"Do you have any idea who did this or why?"

"The only other person that has a key is Finn Morten. I broke up with him last night and forgot to get my spare key back from him before he left. He was pretty angry when he drove away. He tried to call me today, and I didn't answer the phone."

"You broke up with Finn? Good for you. You can do so much better," Sheriff Puckett said, smiling. "I mean, okay, we will check out where he was tonight."

"Can I go in? I didn't go past the front door when I called you. I need to see how extensive the damage is," Tabby requested.

"Yeah, sure. I'll go in with you. I'm sorry. There really isn't much left that's usable," he said, leading the way inside.

Tabby walked from room to room. Tears formed in her eyes as she saw everything she treasured was destroyed. Even her clothes had been ripped beyond use.

"Can you find enough things to pack a small bag? I'd rather you stay in town tonight. I called Miss Jill, and she is going to have a room ready for you at The Sparrow."

"Why would he do this?' Tabby wondered, clutching her grandmother's broken locket.

"Some people don't take rejection well. Finn Morten has a bad temper. I've seen him lose it before. We need to find out where he was tonight. I need to get my men in here to fingerprint and look for anything that would help us to figure out who did this."

"I have extra clothes at Jen's. I'll stop there and pick something up. Let me call her."

Tabby walked to her car and dialed her best friend's number. As she began to tell Jen what happened tears started trickling down her face. She broke the connection and headed back into her apartment.

"I'm going to stay with Jen tonight. I don't want to be alone, even at The Sparrow. If one of you followed me to her place, I would be grateful."

"I will call Miss Jill and cancel the room. Deputy Small will follow you to Jen's house. Do you have a key that I can use to get back in here in the morning? I want you to stay in town tomorrow to give us a chance to finish processing the place. I will notify you when the apartment will be available to you, all right?"

"I'll be at the cable company if you learn anything. Jen said I could stay there as long as I need to. Here is my key. It is the only one I have. Thanks for the escort."

"Just one more quick question. Did you notice anything missing while you were walking around?" Sheriff Puckett asked.

"I honestly couldn't tell in all that mess. I'm sorry."

"That's okay. I will talk to you tomorrow. Small, make sure she gets inside before you leave," Puckett ordered.

"Come on, Tabs, we'll get you safely to Jen's," he said. "We'll get whoever did this. Don't you worry."

Tabby crawled in her car, started it, and pulled out of the parking lot with the cruiser close in tow. Neither of them noticed a small black car tucked back in the brush on the side of the road just outside the Starling parking lot. The man hiding in the darkness was intently watching the chaos at Tabby's apartment.

When they arrived in town, Jen met her best friend at the door. She hugged her tight and led her inside where Samantha Moon was anxiously waiting for her daughter. Tabby finally broke down and cried for over an hour as her mom hugged her and Jen made her a cup of tea.

"I knew he was trouble," Samantha stewed, brushing away her daughter's tears. "They'll catch him. Try not to worry."

"I'm so scared, Mom," Tabby lamented. "He destroyed everything I own. It's like he was out of control with rage."

"You aren't going back there. We already talked to Mr. Wells, and he wants you to stay in town," Jen said.

"I have almost nothing left. He even destroyed my furniture and clothes," Tabby sobbed. "I didn't have renter's insurance either."

"Don't you worry about it tonight. Sheriff Puckett wants me to bring you out there tomorrow to help him go through things. We'll see if anything can be saved. Jen made up the spare bed for you. Try and get some rest and I will be over early in the morning to help you," Samantha assured her, standing to leave.

"I love you. I should have listened to you earlier," Tabby whispered, hugging her mom.

"We all have to learn in our own time. Get some sleep. Jen, thank you so much for helping us out. My place isn't big enough for two people. I'll see you both in the morning."

Samantha left, and Jen locked the door and dead-bolted it after her. She did the same thing to the back door. Tabby sat there drinking her tea and wondered how something like this could happen in Whipper Will Junction? Then again, Finn wasn't from Whipper Will Junction. He was born and raised in the city of Larsen. A local wouldn't have done this to another local.

"Your mom already called your boss and told him you wouldn't be in tomorrow. He said to tell you he was sorry and to take as much time off as you need," Jen relayed, sitting in the chair opposite her friend.

"I don't get it. I gave Finn everything for the last six years. He was furious, but I can't believe he would do something like this to me."

"You never know. He couldn't live in his own house because it was full to the rafters with junk, so when you kicked him out, you took away his place to lounge and his free food. He has to fend for himself now, and I don't think he likes that idea. Sheriff Puckett will figure this out. If you think about it, who else could it be besides Finn? Everyone else in this town likes and respects you."

"I know everything points to Finn. This started out as such a great day and now this. Thanks for letting me stay here. Do you mind if I go to bed? I'm exhausted."

"Do you think I would have let you stay anywhere else? You're in the spare bedroom and are welcome to stay as long as you need to. I'll have coffee ready for you in the morning. Good night."

Tabby lay in bed staring at the ceiling. There was silence. At night, the center of town was just as quiet as living outside of town. She realized that living above her store was going to be okay.

A black car drove up Main Street, idling in front of the book store. The man stared up at the second floor and punched the steering wheel out of sheer frustration. He pulled away and continued down Main Street.

Tabby heard the car leaving. Thinking it might be Finn looking for her, she got up and peered out the window. All she could see was the back end of a small black car disappearing behind the trees that lined the street. It wasn't Finn's truck. Relief slowed her heartbeat, and she was able to go back to bed and fall into a dead man's sleep. This entire weekend had been way too much for her to handle.

4

Samantha pulled up in front of the book store and beeped. Tabby came out, coffee in hand, and climbed in beside her mom.

"Are you ready for this? The sheriff's been out at your place since sun-up. He called me to make sure we were coming."

"Yeah, I guess. I just want to get it over with. Do you know what's lousy, Mom?" Tabby sighed. "I am going to have to use the money I had saved to open my store to replace all my household items and clothes. I won't be able to open my store until next year. I saved for three years to make Jellies, Jams, and Weddings happen, and now it's gone."

"Let's wait and see how much we can save from your apartment before you declare a total loss," her mom suggested.

"You didn't see it, everything was destroyed. There's nothing left to salvage."

They pulled into the Starling Apartments, and the sheriff's cruiser was parked in front of Tabby's place. The other residents were milling about trying to see inside. Gladys Twittle was sitting in her car watching everything.

"Now why doesn't that surprise me?" Tabby asked, pointing out Gladys to her mother.

"You know how she is. She thinks she has to know everything that happens in this town. Don't let her get to you. Let's give her a little wave. Ready?" Samantha quipped, waving, and steering her daughter toward the open door of the apartment.

"I'm glad you're here," the sheriff stated.

"Have you found anything, Stan?" Samantha inquired, looking around in disbelief.

"Truthfully, nothing so far. We dusted for fingerprints and sent them off to the lab. Finn's prints are on record from a previous altercation. Tabby, you will need to go down to the station so we can rule your fingerprints out as well. I have never seen anything like this before. I just have a funny feeling this wasn't done out of anger. It's almost like someone was looking for something."

"Oh, no," Tabby cried out, running off.

The others followed her as she ran to the corner of her bedroom where her grandmother's stuffed animal collection was. They were all scattered on the floor. Some of them had their heads ripped off, and others were sliced open with a knife. Tabby dropped to the floor pushing heads and bodies aside looking for something specific.

"What are you doing?" he asked.

"My grandmother's ring was hidden inside Bathroom Bear. Finn knew I had the ring and how much it was worth, but he didn't know where it was hidden."

"What is a Bathroom Bear?" the sheriff queried.

"It's a stuffed bear that is dressed in a bathrobe and has curlers on its head. One of its hands is holding a toothbrush," Tabby acknowledged, searching frantically.

"How much is the ring worth?"

"We had it appraised two years ago, and they put a value on it of twelve thousand dollars," Samantha confirmed. "It has a center one-carat ruby with two surrounding one-carat diamonds set in platinum."

They all started searching for the bear. The sheriff held up an arm holding a toothbrush.

"Is this part of the bear?"

Tabby shook her head yes, and they kept looking. Under a

Jellies, Jams, and Bodies

comforter in the hallway, the sheriff found the headless, one-armed body of Bathroom Bear. Tabby ran over and grabbed it from him and pushed aside the bathrobe to stick her finger up the remaining arm.

"Is it there?" her mom asked, holding her breath.

Her daughter held up a pink tissue folded into a small square.

"He didn't find it, Mom!" she exclaimed. "It's still here."

"Samantha, why don't you take Tabby out to the car and let her sit for a while," the sheriff suggested.

"No. I need to look for a couple more things. I noticed Gram's locket last night. The chain was broken, but I think it can be repaired."

The sheriff brought in a box from his car and set it near the front door. Tabby walked around and collected what could be salvaged. Some books, a few scarves, and a couple of board games were added to the box. Silverware, pans, and a heavy wooden cutting board was all that could be saved in the kitchen. Even her toaster and blender had been smashed to pieces on the floor. She walked back to the bedroom followed by her mother.

"Some of the clothes in your bureau can be saved. Do you want them?" Samantha asked, holding up some socks and underwear.

"He touched them. He went through all my personal things. I can't wear them again, Mom, I just can't," Tabby responded with a shiver.

"It's okay, I completely understand," she acknowledged, tossing the clothes back in the drawer.

Tabby found the locket exactly where she had dropped it the night before. She slid it in her front jean's pocket where she could keep it close. They wandered back to the living room where the sheriff was standing next to Mr. Wells who had just shown up.

"Tabby, I am so sorry. I want you to take whatever you want to save from here today. I have contracted a cleaning company to come here tomorrow to clean out the unit. I don't want you to have to deal with it," Richard Wells said, giving her a hug.

"That's very kind of you, Richard," Samantha affirmed, giving him a quick kiss on the cheek. "My daughter is having such a tough time with this."

"Thank you so much," Tabby acknowledged, returning his hug. "I guess it's a good thing that I talked you into renting me the other place."

"I will feel much better with you in town where everyone can keep an eye on you," the elderly gentleman added.

"I'll feel much better, too. Until they locate Finn and find out if it was him that did this, I will feel safer being up on the second floor," Tabby agreed.

"Is there any question whether it was her boyfriend or not?"

"I don't know for certain, Richard. Call it a hunch, but I don't believe it was Finn. I think it was someone else."

"Keep on top of it. I've got to head out. I have an appointment with my attorney to go after Fink. I think he's been falsifying the books for all my rentals."

"Thanks again," Samantha said as he walked out the door.

The rest of the morning was spent rifling through the mess that used to be Tabby's home. She found small items here and there that she wanted to take with her for sentimental reasons. The one box was almost full when Tabby and her mother finished going through the last room.

They had noticed that Gladys, the town snoop, had left at eight-thirty. The antique shop opened at nine, and she had to be there to man the counter. The stories were probably flying out of Gladys's mouth even though she really didn't know anything. But she was great at convincing the other locals that she did.

"Are you hungry?" her mom asked.

"A little, I guess," Tabby answered, placing what remained of her life in the trunk of the car.

"Want to go to the Outdoor Café for a quick lunch?" Samantha inquired as she started the car.

"Sure. It's not like I have to go to work today. I would like to spend some time this afternoon cleaning the apartment over the shop. If I stick to the schedule I had laid out in my head, I will only have to stay at Jen's for a little over a week."

They spent the next hour eating, talking, and laughing. Tabby felt much better after spending time with her mom. They were sharing a

Jellies, Jams, and Bodies

strawberry shortcake with extra whipped cream when Samantha's cellphone rang.

That's groovy. I'll be there shortly, and thank you so, so much.

"Who was that?" Tabby asked.

"It was Judy Lovette. She has an extra queen-size bed stored in her attic that she wants you to have for your new place. It doesn't have a mattress, but it does have a box spring. I've seen the bed, and it is drop-dead gorgeous. I think it's what they call a sleigh bed. We can get you a new mattress next week. What do you think?"

"That is so thoughtful of Judy. I've never had a bed with an actual headboard before. Things are looking up already," Tabby smiled as she plopped a big ripe strawberry in her mouth.

They finished their dessert and Samantha paid the bill. Opening all the windows in the car, they cranked up the radio and headed for town.

"Can you drop me off at Mac's, please?" Tabby requested. "I need to buy some more cleaning supplies to get started on the new apartment this afternoon."

"Sure, hon, not a problem."

As they hit the edge of town, Samantha drove right past the market.

"Mom, I asked you to drop me off at Mac's. Hello?"

Her mom kept driving until she pulled into a space in front of the soon to be baseball shop. There was a group of women standing around on the sidewalk. Tabby recognized most of the women as locals and friends to her and her mom. As they stepped out of the car, the women rushed over to meet them, giddy with excitement.

"Surprise," Judy Lovette, one of the owners of The Sparrow Bed and Breakfast said. "Come with us."

Tabby followed Judy and the rest of the women to the rear of the building. They stopped at the stairs that led up to Tabby's new place.

"Go ahead. It's unlocked," Gloria Puckett, the sheriff's wife instructed.

"I don't understand," Tabby confessed, looking at one familiar face and then another.

They were all smiling and very dirty. It hit her all at once.

"You didn't... did you?" she asked, turning to run up the stairs.

As Tabby opened the door to the apartment the pungent smell of pine cleaner and bleach crinkled her nose. She ran from room to room checking things out. The entire apartment had been cleaned from top to bottom. There was not a speck of dirt or dust to be found anywhere. The new sleigh bed had been set up in the bedroom. She hurried down the stairs to the group of women below and hugged each one of them as she thanked them.

"I can't believe this," Tabby sputtered. "Mom, you knew?"

"It was my job to keep you away for the morning. Gloria called me last night, and since she has the phone tree numbers for the Brown Bear Lodge, she had all of this organized before you were even in bed."

"Now you can go shopping this weekend for your new place instead of cleaning it," Betsy Lord, co-owner of Chocolate Motion, suggested.

Tabby's smile turned to a frown.

"What's the matter?" Betsy asked. "Did I say something wrong?"

"No, you didn't. I realized last night I have to spend the money I saved to open my store. It's the only way I can replace everything I lost. It will take me another year or so to save the money again. Jellies, Jams, and Weddings won't open this year, but that doesn't take away from the wonderful gift you all gave to me today. I don't know how to thank you."

"We take care of our own around here. We know you would be right in there returning the favor if something happened to someone else. This town is one big family. You and your mom are part of that family," Gloria insisted.

"I don't know about the rest of you, but I need a shower. I will see everyone tomorrow," Betsy inserted.

The group dispersed with Tabby thanking everyone again as they left.

"Were you surprised?" her mom asked.

"Totally," Tabby responded. "This is one of the reasons I love this town and its people."

"Mr. Pierce even made sure that he finished emptying the place before the women got here this morning," her mom added. "I think that Richard called him last night."

I bet he didn't want anyone to see what he had up there. He had to move the telescope.

"Do you want to go shopping this coming weekend? I can get Rosie to watch the shop for me."

"Sounds good. I have to go back to work tomorrow, and I'll stay at Jen's the rest of this week until I have some furniture in my new place. I'll give you a call if something happens and plans change," Tabby said. "I'm going back upstairs to walk around in my clean apartment and make a list of what I need to get. Love you."

Tabby began writing down all the things she needed. The necessities had to be bought first—coffee maker, dishes, bath towels, and sheets. These were just some of the everyday items you use without even thinking about it. As she walked around, she heard loud yelling coming from downstairs.

"I definitely need a couple of rugs to insulate the upstairs from the downstairs noise," she mumbled.

She stopped walking, laid down and put her ear to the floor. Two male voices were in a heated argument in the shop downstairs. Tabby could only catch words here and there of the disagreement.

"Something… something… driving… something."

"Liar… something… files… something… something… guilty… something."

"Get out of my shop, you crook."

The last words were loud and clear enough for Tabby to hear.

A door slammed downstairs. Tabby ran to the front window to see if she could determine who was leaving the shop. There were too many people walking on Main Street for her to know who came out. She stood in the window thinking. A minute later Mr. Pierce exited the shop with a black briefcase in his hand. Tabby watched him drive away in the direction of Larsen.

Well, wasn't that was interesting? It seems our Mr. Pierce does know someone else in Whipper Will Junction after all.

Tabby walked down the adjoining stairs to see if she could gain access to the space below. The door was not locked, and it opened easily as she stepped into the store.

I'll just take a quick look around.

Mr. Pierce had started to put his merchandise up on shelves that had been installed since Tabby had last visited the space. The telescope was sitting in the back room. Next to it sat a tape recorder hooked up to some kind of listening device.

What or who are you listening to, Mr. Pierce?

A noise at the front door warned her that she had to get out of there. Tabby had just enough time to slip behind the door that led back upstairs before Mr. Pierce walked by it. She heard footsteps go down the cellar stairs. Now was her chance to get back to her apartment undetected. She let out a breath of relief when she was standing safely in her own kitchen.

Tabby exited the building by the outside back stairs. Mr. Pierce would never know she had even been there which was a good thing. She could keep an eye on what was going on in the shop, and he wouldn't know he was being watched.

Jen was already home when Tabby arrived.

"Is it already after six?" Tabby asked, looking at her watch.

"It's six-twenty. Where have you been?" Jen quizzed, uncorking a bottle of wine. "Want a glass?"

"Absolutely! I've been to the new apartment."

"How did you like the surprise? I wanted to help but Sienna was in school, and I didn't have anyone to watch the shop. Did the place come out nice?"

"They did such an awesome job! The only thing it needs now is a fresh coat of paint. I will be heading over to the hardware store tomorrow during lunch to pick out some colors," Tabby replied. "I hope to be in my new place by next week."

"I told you that there is no need to rush. It's kind of fun having someone to talk to and share a glass of wine with after work."

"I appreciate that," Tabby responded. "Not to change the subject, but guess what happened today while I was at the new apartment?"

"Do I really want to know?" Jen asked, frowning.

"Mr. Pierce and another man were having a huge argument downstairs. I was trying to listen through the floor but could only pick out

Jellies, Jams, and Bodies

words here and there. Driving, files, and liar were the only words that I could pick out. They were pretty mad at each other."

"Please tell me you didn't go down and get involved," Jen challenged, sipping her wine.

"No, certainly not while they were down there anyway. I tried to see out the front window who had left the store after the argument, but there were too many people on the street to tell who it was. Mr. Pierce stormed out right after the other person left. I did go down after everyone was gone and thankfully Mr. Pierce hadn't put a padlock on the connecting door yet."

"I can't believe it. You're not even moved in yet, and this happens. Have you noticed that trouble follows you everywhere you go?"

"It's not trouble. It's more of a mystery. I'd love to know who the second man was," Tabby replied, ignoring her friend's comments. "And guess what else I found?"

"What?" Jen asked, refilling her wine glass.

"The other day when I was up checking the apartment for the first time, I saw a telescope hidden under a blanket. Mr. Pierce has been watching something or someone out the front window. Today it was moved to the back room of the shop along with a tape recorder attached to some kind of listening device."

"Do you think the shop is a cover and he's there for some other reason?" Jen queried.

"I don't know, but it's pretty weird," Tabby answered. "I'm going to nose around some more and see what I can find out."

"Be careful," her friend warned. "I haven't cooked anything for supper yet. How would you feel about some BLTs?"

"I'm up for that. Want me to cook the bacon?"

"No, I have microwave bacon. It's faster and easier. Sandwiches in five," Jen announced, heading into the kitchen.

The friends chattered through supper and then polished off the bottle of wine together. After the meal and the wine, they were both ready for bed by ten.

Tabby awoke to the savory smell of coffee brewing. Jen had been up since six because she had errands to run before she had to open her book store at eight. Tabby sat down at the kitchen table with her coffee and glanced at the clock on the wall. It was close to seven, so she had some time to relax before her workday began at eight.

"I'm heading out. See you tonight and for heaven's sake try to stay out of trouble, okay?" Jen suggested as she walked out the door laughing.

"How can I get into trouble at work?" Tabby yelled, with a grin on her face.

Even as silence greeted her question, Tabby knew that Jenny was looking out for her. If there was one person in this town who would always have her back, it was Jenny—even more so than Tabby's mom.

She finished her coffee and hopped in the shower. Tabby realized that she would have to wear jeans to work today since it was the only outfit she had left after the burglary. The cable company had a strict uniform of black slacks. You could wear any top as long as it was decent looking and didn't show too much cleavage. Her boss would have to live with the jeans until Tabby could go shopping on Saturday.

She dragged her feet going to work. Up until Sunday night, Tabby had only five more months of working at the cable company. She was going to leave the job at the beginning of September to open her shop on October first. Now she was stuck working at a job she hated for at least another year until she could raise money to replace what she had to spend. It was so depressing. Why did Finn have to be such a jerk?

The air conditioning was running, and the customer service area was already chilly. Tabby pulled her sweater off the hook with a heavy sigh. She half expected Mr. MacAvey to be waiting at the counter. She wasn't there yesterday to help him straighten out his bill so no doubt he would return today. He was one of a handful of customers that only trusted Tabby to fix their billing mistakes. But the place was empty. Patti wasn't even at the second window yet. Tabby sat in her chair at the first window and began counting her money drawer.

Patti and her dad, Mr. Fitch, the owner of the cable company, came walking out of his office together. Mr. Fitch was carrying a large glass pickle jar that was filled with money. They sauntered over to Tabby and placed it on the counter in front of her.

Jellies, Jams, and Bodies

"What's going on?" Tabby asked, closing her money drawer.

"This is all for you," Patti replied, breaking into a huge smile.

"Excuse me?" Tabby questioned in disbelief.

"You know how Monday is always the busiest day of the week? We put out this jar yesterday for donations to help you get a new start. Word got around, and most of the town came in to donate to you. I don't know how much is in there, but it should give you a good start in replacing what you need," Mr. Finch beamed.

"I don't know what to say."

"Your mom mentioned that you had to spend your shop money to replace everything. Everyone in town is looking forward to your new shop opening. They know how hard you have worked and saved for it. Now you won't have to delay anything. Even though I am losing a great employee, I donated too," Mr. Finch said, smiling.

"And I'm losing a fun coworker," Patti mourned.

Tabby hugged them both.

"I don't know what to say, I am absolutely stunned!" Tabby declared.

"Take your jar and set it under the counter. I don't think there will be many customers coming in here today as they all made it a point to stop by and contribute yesterday. One of you can take the day off if you want. I will leave it up to you to talk it over between you and decide. I'm going to get coffee. Anyone want any?" Mr. Fitch asked.

"I'm good," Tabby answered.

"Me, too. Thanks anyway," Patti responded.

"Okay. I'll be back... sometime."

Walking out the door, he left Tabby and Patti to sit at the counter waiting for customers to show up. An hour passed and it was still quiet.

"Do you want to go home?" Tabby inquired.

"I do have errands I could run," Patti declared. "I'll take an extended lunch and check back later. Is that okay with you?"

"Sure, have fun," Tabby said, pulling her already started list from her purse.

She realized she could extend her list from necessary things to things she actually wanted. The pickle jar was resting at her feet filled to the brim with money. She wanted so badly to count it to see how much

45

was in there but didn't think it was the time or the place to do so. It would have to wait until she got home tonight. A piece of paper caught her eye in the middle of the cash. She opened the jar and pulled it out. Mr. Wells had dropped a check into the jar made out to Tabby in the amount of one thousand dollars.

Oh, no. I can't accept this. I need to return this check to him as soon as possible.

She turned the jar around in her hands. There was everything from pennies to hundred-dollar bills in there. The folks in this town had surely gone out of their way to make her feel loved and respected. How could she ever repay everything that had been done for her in the last three days?

The little bell over the door jingled letting Tabby know someone had entered the lobby. She quickly put the jar on the floor so it was hidden. She looked up, and Finn was standing on the other side of the counter.

"You need to leave immediately," Tabby stated in her best no-nonsense voice.

"Not until I talk some sense into you," Finn replied, leaning over the counter into her personal space.

"After what you did Sunday night do you think I even want to talk to you?" Tabby screamed. "Get out! I'll call the sheriff if you don't leave right now!"

"I don't know what you are talking about. What did I supposedly do on Sunday night?"

"You destroyed my apartment. Don't play stupid, Finn. You are the only other person besides me who has a key," Tabby answered, picking up the phone.

"I was visiting my brother in Portland. I just got back to Whipper Will Junction an hour ago. I had to get away from here for a few days to calm down. Your apartment was wrecked?"

"It was totally destroyed. Are you saying you didn't do it?" Tabby questioned, setting down the phone.

"I swear it wasn't me. I wouldn't do something like that to you," Finn replied honestly.

"Finn Morten, hands on the counter. Don't move," Sheriff Puckett yelled, storming through the front door.

"What? What the…" Finn asked as the sheriff rushed him.

He was forced against the counter and placed in handcuffs.

"Sheriff, hold on. Finn said he didn't do it. He was in Portland with his brother all weekend," Tabby stated, coming out from behind the counter.

"It's true. I wouldn't destroy Tabby's stuff. And I *was* in Portland all weekend. I just got back," Finn repeated.

"Until we can verify what you say, you'll have to come down to the station. Deputy, take Mr. Morten to the cruiser."

Tabby watched as Finn was seated in the back of the cruiser. The deputy drove off toward town.

"How did you know Finn was here?" Tabby questioned the sheriff.

"Patti was leaving and saw him pull into the parking lot. She knew you were in here by yourself, so she called me. We'll have to verify if he was actually in Portland and if we can do that, he will be free by early evening."

"If Finn was at his brother's, that will leave us with nothing as to who wrecked my apartment or why."

"I had a funny feeling about this from the beginning. If you remember, I said it looked more like someone was searching for something. I know Finn has a bad temper. I've seen it. But that wreckage was even more than Finn's temper could manage. You be careful, young lady."

"I will. I am still staying at Jen's place. At least until I have furniture in my new place."

Patti came rushing through the door.

"Are you okay? I saw Finn and…"

"I'm fine. Relax."

"Sheriff, will you please let me know if Finn was telling the truth or not. If he was, I guess I'll have to start looking over my shoulder and being more attentive to who and what's around me."

"I'll give you a call as soon as I know anything," he confirmed, walking out the door.

"Are you sure you'll be okay here alone the rest of the day?" Patti queried.

"I'll be fine," Tabby insisted. "No one but Finn has come in yet."

"Okay, call me if you need me," Patti replied.

Just two customers had shown up by closing time. Both came in just to contribute money to the jar. Tabby was embarrassed to hand it to them while she stood watching, but they didn't seem to care.

Just accept everything given to you with a smile. Maybe when your shop opens you can fill little jars and hand them out to the locals as a thank you gift. Just a thought.

At five o'clock, Tabby locked the front door and flipped the sign to closed.

Another day is done. Now, I can go home and count the money in the pickle jar. It's been driving me crazy all day.

Jen would be at work until her shop closed at six o'clock. Tabby had her own key to let herself in. She sat on her bed in the spare room and dumped out the pickle jar. Money went everywhere. She set aside the check from Mr. Wells with the full intention of returning it. She would not include the amount of the check in the final total.

An hour later she had a total—two thousand, one hundred, twenty-eight dollars and eleven cents. She leaned back against her pillows staring at the piles of money. The front door closed with a bang. Tabby left her bedroom to see what was happening. Jen was leaning against the counter in the kitchen, frowning.

"What's the matter? You look like you are *not* a happy camper."

"Larry Fink came into my book store today. He said the taxes went up on the building for the new fiscal year and he needed a check for one hundred and seventy-nine dollars by Friday. I can't come up with that much extra money on top of the rent. Besides, I already paid this year's taxes."

"That's weird because Larry Fink isn't in charge of Mr. Well's rentals anymore. I think we need to pay a visit to our elderly friend and tell him about this new tax rate. He didn't even know that Fink had raised all the rental rates on his properties. He's going to love this one."

"I don't get it. The tax rate went up last year, but my taxes on the building only increased fourteen dollars. This large amount makes no sense at all."

"Let me show you something unbelievable, and then we'll go pay Mr. Wells a visit. My bet is he doesn't know anything about this so-called tax rate increase."

Tabby led her friend into the spare room where the bed was covered in small piles of money.

"Did you rob a bank?" Jen asked in amazement, walking toward the bed.

"Mr. Finch put a big pickle jar out at the cable company, and people came in all day donating money to help me begin again. Is that not classic?"

"How much is there?"

"A little over two thousand dollars. It's a good thing we are going to see Mr. Wells. I have a check I need to return to him—a thousand-dollar check. He has done too much for me already," Tabby said, tucking the check in her back pocket. "You ready? We'll take my car."

Richard Wells lived on the outskirts of town. As much as he loved everyone in Whipper Will Junction, he loved his privacy more. Beaver Creek Road was located a mile past the Starling Apartments. Tabby saw the blue dumpster in front of her old apartment. She was happy that she didn't have to deal with cleaning out the space she used to occupy. It still gave her the shivers knowing someone had gone through all her personal things and if it turned out not to be Finn who destroyed the place, it was even worse.

Mr. Wells' house was the only residence located on Beaver Creek. They pulled up in front of his log cabin. The lights were on inside. The girls stepped up onto the wrap-around porch and noticed the front door was slightly ajar. Calypso was meowing loudly inside.

5

"Mr. Wells, it's Tabby and Jen. Are you home?" Tabby called out as she peeked in the open door. "Hello?"

They stepped inside. The television was on, dinner was on the table, and there was a well-stoked fire roaring in the fireplace. Calypso, Mr. Well's cat, was sitting on the rug in front of the fire.

"Mr. Wells, are you here?" Tabby yelled out.

No answer.

"I don't like this. We'd better take a look around. He might have fallen and hurt himself," Tabby suggested.

The girls walked around the entire cabin. Tabby took a flashlight out of her purse and strolled around outside, calling the elderly gentleman's name. He was nowhere to be found. His car was in the driveway so he couldn't have wandered anywhere. The closest place was a half a mile away. Besides, he had lived here long enough to know not to roam around the woods after dark as there was too much wildlife out there that could be dangerous.

"I don't like this. We need to call the sheriff," Tabby declared, pulling out her cell phone.

Jen had closed the front door so the cat wouldn't get out. She nodded her head in agreement.

"We'll wait right here" Tabby stated. "How long do you think you'll be?"

Calypso was rubbing against Tabby's leg, so Jen picked up the cat and softly spoke to her. The purring could be heard across the room.

"Okay. Thanks."

"He's coming?" Jen asked.

"He'll be here in twenty."

The girls decided to keep searching until the sheriff arrived, but it appeared that nothing was out of place. There were a bunch of papers on the table next to the uneaten dinner. Tabby flipped through them and realized that most of them had to do with his properties. She picked up one item that didn't seem to fit in with the rest. It wasn't a document. It was a blueprint of The Whipper Will Drive-In.

Why would he be interested in the drive-in property? He doesn't even own it.

They saw the headlights of an approaching car. Standing at the front door, holding the cat, they waited to see who it was. It pulled up to the porch, and they could see the dome lights on top of the car. As Sheriff Puckett stepped out of the car, Tabby opened the front door and let him in.

"We have to stop meeting like this," he said to Tabby, chuckling. "Where is Richard?"

"We don't know. The front door was ajar when we arrived, and his supper is on the table, but it looks untouched."

"His car is in the driveway. Let me call his cell."

"You have his cell phone number? He doesn't give that out to anyone!" Jen exclaimed.

"I'm the sheriff, I have everyone's numbers," he responded, punching the little squares on his cell phone.

As he put the phone to his ear, a ringing could be heard coming from the kitchen. Mr. Well's phone was sitting on the counter right next to the stove.

"I don't like this. I have told Richard not to go anywhere without his cell phone. Have you girls touched anything in here?"

"The doorknobs," Tabby answered. "I flipped through the papers on the table. We haven't touched anything else but Calypso."

"I'm going to call my deputies. We need to search the surrounding woods. You girls head home, but be careful."

"Sheriff, did you clear Finn's story?" Tabby inquired.

"Yes, we did. I just hadn't had time to call you to let you know. He was seen by at least a dozen people at a bar on Sunday night. Finn didn't wreck your place. Between that and now this, something is going on in Whipper Will Junction and I don't like it one bit," the sheriff stated.

"Calypso has been fed and has plenty of water. If you don't find Mr. Wells right away, call me, and I will come get the cat. She shouldn't be left here by herself in case someone returns," Jen offered.

"Hopefully, it won't come to that. But, thanks. I'll keep that in mind," the sheriff said.

The girls drove up Beaver Creek passing the deputies on their way to the cabin. Tabby suddenly had a horrific thought and punched the steering wheel hard, scaring Jen.

"Why did you do that?"

"I just remembered. I left all that money laying on the bed right there in the open! With everything that has been going on around here, that was a really stupid thing to do," Tabby admitted, mad at herself for being so careless.

"I set the alarm before we left."

"You have an alarm upstairs?"

"Yes, I have a two-part system—downstairs in the bookstore and upstairs in the apartment. There are too many tourists around in the summer season not to have an alarm system in place. You'll need one, too."

"That makes me feel better. I was still an idiot."

"Yes, you were," Jen smiled.

"You didn't have to agree so fast."

"We can't disagree all the time," Jen said. "So, what do you think happened to Mr. Wells?"

"I don't know. Why would someone just up and leave their supper?

Plus he would never leave the door open for Calypso to get out with all the coyotes around at night. It doesn't look good, I'm afraid."

"What is happening to our quiet little town?" Jen wondered, shaking her head.

They parked in back of the bookstore. Everything was quiet in the center of town. Jen turned off the alarm and Tabby hustled to her bedroom. Thankfully, the money was still on the bed right where she had left it.

So stupid.

She put the sorted money in an envelope and tucked it into her purse. The money would be deposited in the bank before she went to work in the morning.

"I set the alarm so don't go sneaking off in the middle of the night," Jen instructed, smiling. "I'm going to bed. It's been a long day. See you for coffee."

"Night. I have no plans of going anywhere but to bed. Hey Jen, thanks."

"Any time, girlfriend, any time."

The rest of the week passed quickly and without any word on Mr. Wells. Samantha Moon pulled up in front of the bookstore on Saturday morning and beeped. Tabby came jogging out, list in hand, ready to go marathon shopping in Larsen. Her mom had emptied the Mystic Happening's cargo van for the trip. They could shop all day and not fill the van, even if they bought furniture. A mattress was one of the first things on the list.

Tabby had been looking forward to spending time with her mom as it didn't happen very often. Today was the start of a new life, new everything. Plus, what girl doesn't love to go shopping? She didn't have to worry about how much she was spending because of the generosity of all the locals. But that didn't mean she could buy things on a whim either. Smart shopping was her motto for the day.

"Mom, did you hear about Mr. Wells?" Tabby inquired.

"Yes, Gladys was running her almighty mouth at the coffee shop the other morning. She makes up so much stuff that someday someone is going to catch her lying. What is the real story? Word is you and Jen were out at the house."

"We found the front door open and called the sheriff when we couldn't find Mr. Wells anywhere in the cabin. When we left, Sheriff Puckett and his deputies were going to check the surrounding woods. I probably should have called him before we left to see if they had found out anything yet."

"I talked to the sheriff at the coffee shop this morning. They still haven't found him. He was going to call Jen to see if she could pick up Calypso after work. She agreed and is going to meet him out there since he has keys to the house."

"Good. I don't want Jen going there by herself. I sure do hope Mr. Wells is okay."

"This town used to be so quiet. What is happening around here that is causing such an uproar?"

"I don't know, but while we are in Larsen, I want to stop at Rose Point Realty and talk to Lisa Carver. Maybe she knows where Mr. Wells is or has heard from him."

"Don't go sticking your nose in where it doesn't belong, missy. You have a bad habit of doing that," her mother warned.

"I won't, I promise," Tabby said.

"I've heard that promise before," Samantha stated, rolling her eyes.

The rest of the day was spent traveling from store to store buying everything Tabby needed to start over. The mattress fit in the van but didn't leave room for the other big pieces of furniture she bought. The furniture store agreed to deliver a couch, a matching recliner, and two bureaus on Monday. Every other purchase was stuffed in the van until it was ready to burst.

Tabby purchased a new wardrobe including undergarments, socks, and sandals. She would pick up other clothes as the seasons changed. Samantha spent time and money shopping at the Larsen Paranormal Experience for replacement stock for her small shop.

The twosome had lunch at the Larsen Tropical Café. Tabby ordered the biggest burger they had on the menu, loaded with bacon, cheese, pickles, tomatoes, and Russian dressing. Samantha stuck with her usual salad. She hadn't touched red meat for many years and couldn't watch as her daughter ate the burger. Tabby couldn't resist teasing her mother by moaning and making other noises of pure enjoyment while she ate the whole burger right down to the last pickle.

"Sometimes I don't think you're my child at all," her mom stated woefully, finishing her salad.

"Let's stop at the realty company next," Tabby suggested, paying the lunch bill.

Samantha stayed in the car while Tabby went in to talk to Lisa Carver. She was directed to a desk in the rear of the office where Miss Carver was on the phone. Tabby waited for her to finish. She couldn't help but stare at the agent. There was something familiar about her.

Where have I seen her before?

Tabby could tell Miss Carver was uncomfortable with the way she was staring at her. She hurried the phone call along and finally hung up.

"How can I help you?" the agent inquired, standing, and extending her hand.

"My name is Tabitha Moon. I came here from Whipper Will Junction to talk to you about Mr. Wells. Have you talked to my friend lately?"

"I talked to Richard yesterday morning."

"Yesterday morning? That's funny because he's been missing since Tuesday."

"I don't know, maybe it was Tuesday I talked to him. I'm so busy, my days blend together at this job," Lisa confessed.

"Did he seem upset to you when you did talk to him? Did he ask you to take over his rentals from Larry Fink?"

"I cannot discuss my client's private business with other people, let alone someone I don't even know. What is your interest in Mr. Wells' affairs?" Miss Carver asked, herding Tabby closer to the exit door.

"Mr. Wells is missing, and we will find him," Tabby stated flatly, fishing for a reaction.

"Miss Moon, I don't like your questions or your tone of voice. I want you to leave my office and not come back. Do you understand?"

"Oh, I understand perfectly. Have a nice day, Miss Carver."

Jellies, Jams, and Bodies

Tabby crawled up into the van. She plunked down in the seat and crossed her arms.

"I know that look. What happened in there?" her mom asked, frowning.

"I can't shake the feeling that I have seen her somewhere before. She sure didn't like me asking questions about Mr. Wells. She told me she talked to Richard yesterday morning and when I called her on it, she made up a lame excuse that she got her days mixed up. Then, she ordered me to leave her office and not come back. She couldn't get me out of there quick enough."

"I think you need to tell Sheriff Puckett about this," her mom suggested as she started the van. "Why don't you go with Jen to pick up the cat and talk to him then?"

"I think I will," Tabby answered. "Her face was just so familiar to me."

Samantha pulled the van up to the back stairs of Tabby's apartment. They unloaded the van with the exception of the mattress.

"Let me see if Mr. Pierce is in his shop. I'll ask him if he will help us with the mattress," Tabby proposed, walking to the front of the store.

The baseball card shop owner was busy stacking inventory on his shelves. When Tabby knocked on the locked door, Mr. Pierce smiled and walked over to unlock it for her.

"Hello. Tabitha, right?"

"Call me Tabby. Do you have a minute to help my mom and I get a queen-size mattress up the back stairs?"

"Sure, not a problem. Let's go," he answered, leading the way out of the store.

"I really appreciate this," Tabby commented. "Just so you know, I bought some rugs to keep the noise down both upstairs and downstairs muffled. What are your store hours going to be?"

"Nine to five."

"I'll be at work during that time. I guess there will be no noise to bother you or your customers," Tabby offered, giving him her best beaming smile.

"And I won't be around at night while you are home. This will work out perfectly."

Tabby introduced Mr. Pierce to her mother. They chatted for a few minutes, and then the three of them struggled to wrangle the mattress up the stairs.

"Thanks so much," Tabby remarked. "I'll be moving in permanently when the rest of my furniture is delivered."

"When are you opening your store?" Samantha asked.

"Next weekend is the grand opening," Pierce replied.

"You're new to town. Where are you from?" Tabby inquired, being nosy.

"Originally, I am from Portland. I was an airline pilot for 42 years, but last year I decided to retire. Two years ago I came here for vacation and fell in love with the place. I signed a lease with Mr. Wells for one season to see how a baseball card shop would do in the area. I know you have this shop after I'm out, so if I decide to stay in the area, I'll rent the shop at the end of town since it's bigger."

"Well, I wish you luck with your shop," Samantha said, taking out her car keys. "We should have coffee sometime."

"That would be nice," Mr. Pierce agreed, as he turned to leave.

"Thanks again," Tabby said.

"Anytime."

Mr. Pierce returned to his shop, smiling and certain he had covered his tracks.

Tabby checked her watch. She still had half an hour before she had to meet Jen at Mr. Wells' house. She hummed to herself as she made up the bed with her new sheets and the purple satin quilt she had bought. By taking a personal day from work on Monday for the furniture delivery, coupled with her regular weekend days off, she had three days to get her apartment set up the way she wanted it.

Soon the rest of her furniture would be delivered, the cable, the internet, and the phone would be installed, and she could start living her life again. The electricity was already on in the building. She would have to talk to Mr. Pierce to see how they would split the electric bill.

Once her internet was connected, she could order supplies to start stockpiling her jellies inventory. She needed jars and covers, labels, and a bulk order of fruit pectin. She needed to talk to Mac to place special orders for large amounts of strawberries, raspberries, and sugar. She planned to have a couple of batches cooking, with open windows, while Mr. Pierce had his grand opening downstairs.

There was much to do in advance of the store opening. A list of wedding supplies and event connections needed to be finalized. After the furniture was delivered on Monday, Tabby would walk to the flower shop and meet the owner. Her business cards had come in and luckily, she had them mailed to her mother's store, so they weren't destroyed in the break-in.

Tabby met Jen and the sheriff at Mr. Wells' house. She told the sheriff about her meeting with Lisa Carver and how she looked familiar to her somehow. Jen was busy collecting Calypso's toys, and she had already purchased a new litter box earlier in the day.

"You need to be careful, Tabby. We still don't know what happened to Wells," the sheriff warned. "Please, no investigating on your own, not that you have ever listened to me before."

"I'll be careful, but I'm scared for Mr. Wells, and I want to help find him. I just figured that while I was in Larsen, I would drop in and see Miss Carver."

Jen needed help getting the unwilling cat in the carrier. Calypso wanted nothing to do with being confined in a cage, and it took all three of them to corral the cat and finally slide her into the carrier. Accompanied by loud meows, the sheriff carried Jen's new roommate to the car.

Tabby walked over to the dining room table and saw the papers were still there. Once again Tabby picked up the blueprints of the drive-in. They just didn't fit in with all the other papers Mr. Wells had been perusing. She looked the paperwork over carefully. There were no handwriting or handwritten marks on them. Tabby rolled up the blueprint and stuffed it in her purse.

Why are you so interested in the drive-in?

"Are you ready to go?" the sheriff asked, returning from Jen's car.

"Yeah, Jen might need help when the cat is let out of the carrier. She'll probably wait until I get there so we can close and lock the door. Let me know if you find out anything."

Tabby drove off as the sheriff was locking up the house. When she arrived at Jen's, the cat was still hunkered down in the carrier meowing loudly. Tabby locked the door behind her as she stepped into the apartment.

"Are you ready?" Jen asked, unlocking the carrier.

Calypso shot out as soon as the door was opened. She ran behind the couch and wouldn't come out, so Jen set her food bowl at the end of the couch.

"Let's leave her alone. She'll come out when she's good and ready. What do you want for supper?" Jen asked, heading to the kitchen.

"I bought two steaks while I was out," Tabby said. "What about salad and steak?"

"Sounds good to me."

Jen started cooking supper while Tabby laid out the blueprints on the kitchen table.

"What do you know about The Whipper Will Drive-In?" Tabby questioned.

"Not much. I know it is owned by Marsha and Peyton Swanson. Peyton died over the winter in Florida. I guess Marsha owns it now. They are snowbirds like a lot of the business people in this town. What are those?" Jen asked as she wandered over to the table.

"They are blueprints to the drive-in. They were on Mr. Wells' table."

"You took them? Does the sheriff know?"

"Not exactly. I kind of rolled them up and hid them in my purse while he helped you out with the cat."

"Why did you take them?"

"These papers didn't fit in with everything else that was on the table. All the other paperwork dealt with properties that Mr. Wells already owned. He doesn't own the drive-in. I'm sure he wasn't going to buy it. He's retiring to Florida. So why is he interested in that particular property?"

"Good question. Is anything written on the plans? Maybe on the back?" Jen inquired as she set the plates on the kitchen table.

Tabby turned the plans over. In the back-top corner, there was a three-digit number—seven-seven-two, handwritten in red ink. Under the numbers were the initials M.F.C. There was nothing else on the back.

"M.F.C. Could that be a person's initials?" Tabby pondered, thinking out loud.

"I can't think of anyone with those initials in Whipper Will," Jen stated, setting down the rest of supper. "Dinner is served."

The friends ate supper together, cleaned up the dishes and went to bed early since they were scheduled to be greeters at church in the morning. When the lights were turned off, and the house was quiet, Calypso decided to come out from behind the couch and investigate her new surroundings. Tabby could hear the cat eating her crunchy food. Several minutes later, the cat could be heard digging in the litter box in the bathroom.

Tabby lay in bed thinking about the blueprints and Mr. Wells. What could he possibly know that would put his life at risk? She closed her eyes to sort out her thoughts. Calypso jumped up on the bed and settled down next to Tabby's arm and immediately started purring and then drifted off to sleep.

"I guess I have a new friend," she said, scratching the cat's head. "Sleep well. We'll get you home as soon as possible, I promise."

The girls were at the front door greeting the locals as they arrived at church. A couple of them of them whispered to Tabby how happy they were that she was no longer dating Finn as they shook her hand. Jen stifled giggles each time it was said. After the service during coffee hour, the topic of discussion was Richard Wells and what happened to him. Gladys, of course, put her two cents in whenever she could, telling anyone who would listen her theories on the disappearance. Her husband looked on rolling his eyes behind her back.

"I'm going to head out," Tabby stated. "I want to organize my kitchen and closets today. I was going to go to the new flower shop on Monday after my furniture arrived, but I think I'll go down today and introduce myself to the owner. Want me to stop and pick you up when I go?"

"Sure. I haven't seen the new shop yet. I'll be at home spending some time with Calypso and working on my shop books," Jen answered. "See you then."

It was a beautiful day. Tabby took her time walking home, enjoying the warm sunshine on her face. She passed by the front of her building and saw Mr. Pierce was busy setting up his shop for the grand opening. He smiled and waved as she entered the alley that led to the back of the building.

The next two hours Tabby unpacked shopping bags and put things away. Her kitchen still needed a coat of paint, but with everything she had bought, it was starting to look like a usable kitchen. Two large lobster pots that she bought for jelly making took their honored place on the top of the refrigerator.

She moved on to the living room. The ten by twelve-foot rug she purchased for the room fit perfectly. The swirl pattern made up of teals, grays, and blacks would match with the light teal furniture that was being delivered tomorrow. A black wrought-iron clock was hung on the wall above where the television had been placed.

A black, three-tier plant stand was placed in front of the picture window that overlooked the street. Her plants would get plenty of sunshine all day in this spot. She hung several pictures that fit perfectly with the rest of the décor. Tabby looked around and smiled.

This room is straight out of a design magazine. It's beautiful.

She placed the remaining unpacked bags back in the second bedroom. She grabbed a couple of her business cards and tucked them in her purse and left for her friend's apartment. Jen was diligently working at her computer as Tabby interrupted her. Calypso was lying in a sunbeam on the floor next to Jenny's desk. She stretched as Tabby bent down to scratch her behind the ears.

"You ready to go?"

"Yeah, let me get my purse," Jen said, shutting down her computer.

They headed to the front door and noticed that Calypso didn't seem to care that they were leaving. She closed her eyes and fell back to sleep in the warm sun. The cat had settled in nicely after being moved to her new temporary residence.

They walked up Main Street taking notice of what shops were getting ready to open for the season. Tabby made a list as they walked of shops that she would approach to carry her jams and jellies for the summer. There was a sign in the window of *The Local Scoop* that the ice cream shop would be opening soon.

"I know where I'm going to be on opening night," Jen said, licking her lips.

"I'll be right there with you," Tabby agreed.

They reached the end of Main Street. The Smells So Fine Flower Shop was open and very busy. The front picture window contained displays of wedding flowers. Several types of bouquets, table centerpieces and altar arrangements set on white satin filled the window.

"I don't think they are as good as yours," Jen whispered quietly. "Nice, but yours are better."

"Let's go meet the owner and see who makes these arrangements," Tabby suggested, opening the door.

They entered the door and stopped short in their tracks.

"Do you see what I see?" Tabby asked in amazement.

"I don't believe it," Jen sputtered.

6

"That's my frog fountain!" Tabby cried out, running to the back corner of the shop.

"I don't believe this!" Jen exclaimed as she caught up with her friend.

They stood in front of the fountain, staring, neither one could believe it ended up in their own town. Apparently, the owner of the flower shop was the anonymous phone caller that had outbid Tabby. She didn't know whether to be mad at the owner or happy that she could visit it and see it working.

"She's a real beauty, isn't she?" a deep voice asked from behind them.

The friends turned around at the same time.

"Hi, you're new to my shop. I'm Greg Stone, owner of the Smells So Fine Flower Shop."

"You were the mysterious phone bidder," was the only sentence Tabby was capable of uttering.

"Excuse me?" Greg asked, his blue eyes twinkling.

"I was at the auction because I wanted this particular fountain for my own shop. You outbid me," Tabby muttered, cutting the owner a spiteful stare.

"Were you the person bidding against me? You sure drove the price up."

"That was me. I had planned on spending up to four hundred dollars, and you blew me right out of the water with your final bid," Tabby relented with a small smile.

She couldn't help but smile. Greg was gorgeous. Six-foot-tall, the body of a god, and jet-black hair that made his baby blue eyes pop. How could anyone stay mad at someone who looked like that? Tabby stuck her hand out.

"Tabitha Moon. People around here call me Tabby. I will be opening my new shop at the end of September in the center of town. The Baseball Card Shop is there right now, but that will be my storefront soon."

"What kind of shop are you opening?" Greg queried.

"Jellies, Jams, and Weddings. It's a crazy name, but it fits my shop perfectly. Actually, that's why we came in today. I wanted to give you my business card and talk about setting up an account for the wedding aspect of my shop. This is Jen Jones, my best friend."

"Hi, just call me Jen. I own the Until the Book Ends bookstore in the center of town."

"I've been in your book store. A young girl named Sienna was working. I'll be seeing you a lot. I love to read. I can usually go through three or four books a week."

"You should check out our 'Borrow a Book' program. It's pretty cool," Jen suggested.

"Have you found out if the fountain works or not? It looked pretty hosed when I opened it up at the auction," Tabby inquired, moving to the back of the fountain.

"It doesn't work. I had to order a whole new motor. I should have it up and running within a week. Why did you want the fountain so badly, if you don't mind me asking?"

"It was going to be the centerpiece of my shop. I wanted to set a few tables and chairs around it so people could come in, enjoy a cup of coffee, and relax. I saw it in the catalog and had to have it, but *someone* had more money than I did."

"I had the same idea. I wanted people to come in and enjoy the beauty of my flowers."

"I see that. I like the benches set up on either side of the lily pond.

Jellies, Jams, and Bodies

The tall tables look nice around the fountain. I guess great minds think alike," Tabby agreed.

"You and Jen can come visit the frogs anytime you want," Greg teased.

"Greg, I need your help, please," the clerk interrupted their conversation.

"Look around. Drop your business cards at the register. I'll be in touch to set up a meeting to discuss an open-end account for your business. Nice meeting you both," Greg stated as he walked briskly away.

The girls walked around the flower shop checking out the wedding items. They could see an older woman in the back room working on a bridal bouquet.

"She must be Greg's designer," Jen whispered. "Your wedding items are more original. you have a flair for the romantic."

"I heard that," Greg admitted, passing behind them.

"Oh crap," Jen said, making a face. "I didn't know he was near us."

"Me neither. Let's drop our cards off and head out before we annoy him," Tabby suggested.

They gave the two cards to the clerk at the register who introduced herself as Sally Rogers. They waved goodbye as they walked by Greg who was busy helping an older woman. He smiled a big, gorgeous smile and returned his attention to his customer.

"I can truthfully say if I had to lose the frogs to someone, I am glad it was him," Tabby commented. "He is gorgeous."

"He is, and those eyes could melt an iceberg," Jen agreed. "I think he was interested in you, Tabs."

"Yeah, I could be so lucky."

"We'll see just how lucky you are. What do you say we stop at Mac's and get some nice fish for supper?"

"I haven't had fish for ages. Finn wouldn't eat it, and he didn't like it when I cooked it because he said it stunk up the house. How about some swordfish?"

The girls stopped at the market and picked up what they needed for their last supper together before Tabby moved to her new place. Calypso was going crazy from the smell of fish while it cooked, so Jen shared a small piece with the cat while they ate their supper. A bottle of wine later they went to bed.

Monday morning Tabby was up early with Jen so they could enjoy their coffee together. As Jen was getting ready to leave, Tabby hugged her friend and started to cry.

"What is with you?' Jen wondered.

"I'm so lucky to have a best friend like you. You always have my back, no matter what," Tabby sniffled.

"And I always will as long as it's not something dangerous. I'm not as brave as you," her friend said, smiling. "I have to run. The book store won't open itself. Love you, crazy friend!"

"I'll check in with you after the furniture is delivered."

Tabby made sure Calypso had food and water before she left. She was curled up on the window seat in the front window. The cat loved to lay in the sun. Her heart ached looking at the cat. No one had seen or heard from Mr. Wells since the night he went missing. She was worried about her elderly friend and knew he was more than likely worried about his precious companion that had been left behind at the house.

The furniture was delivered at nine o'clock sharp as promised. Two men carried everything up the back stairs and arranged the items in the rooms as she instructed. Tabby looked around after they left. She could hardly believe that this beautiful new home was really hers! In the old apartment, all her household things had been from the thrift store or yard sales. She rarely had money to buy new things. This was such a huge step up in her lifestyle. She had a new home, was starting a new business, and had a lead on a hunky new male friend.

Dom from the cable company showed up at the apartment at noon to install the cable and the internet. His tool belt hung low under his beer belly and made clinking noises as he walked.

"Nice place, Tabby," he offered, running the cable through a hole in the floor. "I need to get in the cellar. Is that going to be a problem?"

"Let me run downstairs and check with Mr. Pierce first. I'll be right back."

She decided to use the indoor stairs that led from her kitchen to the card shop. Her hand was raised to knock on the door when she heard voices raised in a heated argument. They were the same two voices she had heard the other night. She stopped behind the closed door to listen.

I told you before, I don't know what you're talking about.

Liar! I will find it. This is your last warning. Stay out of my way and don't mess in business that doesn't concern you.

Don't threaten me. You are nothing but a low-life scumbag. Richard Wells doesn't trust you, and neither does anyone else. Get out of my shop and don't step foot in here again or there will be consequences.

Tabby ran up the stairs, through the kitchen, and down the back stairs to outside. This time she wasn't going to miss seeing who came out of the shop. She just reached the sidewalk when Larry Fink came storming out the front door. She ducked back around the corner of the building. Fink pulled out his cell phone and was yelling at someone on the other end of his call before he reached his office across the street. He turned as he entered his building and saw Tabby standing there watching him. He scowled and disappeared through the front door.

Tabby knocked on the front door of the shop.

"Go away!"

She knocked again. This time Mr. Pierce came out of the backroom. When he saw it was Tabby, his face softened, and he unlocked the door.

"I'm sorry to bother you, Mr. Pierce. The cable man is here, and he needs to get into the cellar to finish hooking up my service. Is that okay?"

"Yes, of course. Tell him to come right down, the door will be unlocked."

"Thank you. I hope it is not an inconvenience to you."

"Not at all. The shop is almost ready for the grand opening. I have a few last-minute things to do so I'll be in the backroom. Do you know where the cellar stairs are?"

"Yes, I do. We'll be in and out before you know it. I promise," Tabby assured.

Tabby returned to her apartment and told Dom that they had permission to go into the cellar. She led him to the cellar door and opened it. Looking for a light switch, she found and tugged on a pull string at the top of the stairs.

Dom followed Tabby down the old, worn wooden staircase. The cable installer found the old box that had been used by the previous tenants. As he was busy hooking up the wires he sent through the holes in the floor, Tabby took the time to look around the cellar. The baseball shop's inventory was spread around the perimeter, hoisted up on pallets to keep it off the dirt floor. She noticed there was something funny about the walls around the room. It looked like someone had punched holes in various places along both sides and then patched them up.

This is weird.

"That should do it," Dom announced, stretching as he stood up. "All that's left is to program your passcodes in, and you'll be all set."

"Great, thank you so much."

"Looks like someone used the walls down here to let off steam," Dom observed as he looked around the room.

"I know. Weird, huh?" answered Tabby. "Let's go hook up my internet."

Twenty minutes later, Tabby was connected to the cyber world again. She thanked Dom and told him she would see him tomorrow at work.

Once he was gone, she pulled her debit card out of her wallet and settled in to do some serious online shopping. All the supplies she needed for jelly making were ordered with rush shipping. Tabby wanted everything in her hands by the week's end so she could flood Main Street with the wonderful smells of her gram's jams and jellies. Several shops on Main Street were opening this weekend, so there would be a lot of foot traffic in the center of town.

Locals would be welcoming the snowbirds back, and it was April vacation for most school systems in the New England area. The last week in April was the unofficial start to tourist season in Whipper Will Junction. Summer residents came to open up their vacation homes and rental houses. This coming week the tourists would outnumber the locals, and it would stay that way until late October.

Tabby remembered the smells that used to waft through the town when her gram was alive and cooking. The locals treasured her jams and jellies. Her finished products were not like any other out there.

Excitement would build for the first batch of the new season, and her gram would usually sell out within the first hour. That afternoon you could smell the next batch cooking. It got to the point where people would pre-order several jars at a time to keep ahead of the back-up of orders. The local inns and restaurants would put their orders in prior to the start of the season. Tabby was counting on these established orders to help her business take off.

Many people tried to get Gram to tell them the secret ingredients, but she kept it to herself. The recipes were stored in her mind. When she got older and couldn't cook anymore, she wrote the recipes down on paper. The only one to ever see them would be her granddaughter.

Tabby hoped the excitement for the jams and jellies would still be there. She would find out this coming weekend when she cooked the first batch with all her windows open to tempt the shoppers passing by on the street below.

It was shortly after five when Tabby decided to treat herself to supper at the diner since she still hadn't made that trip to the market for her big first grocery purchase. That was on the plan for tomorrow night after work. She changed her clothes and brushed her hair. Samantha Moon had given her daughter an ornate vanity set for her bedroom. Painted in brushed gold, the triple mirror folded outward so the person sitting on the matching bench could see her reflection on all sides. Tabby didn't really care for the gold color of the mirror, and she decided that when she had more time in the fall, she would paint it a color she preferred.

Tabby looked in the mirror. Staring back at her was a pretty woman, not beautiful, but okay looking. Her waist length, auburn hair had just enough wave to it to make the blond highlights stand out. She had green eyes that were the color of shamrock fields that could be seen all over Ireland. She must have inherited her dad's eyes because her moms were dark brown. Five-seven, and a great figure, she could turn heads if she wanted to. She wondered if she could make Greg's head turn her way.

What are you thinking? You don't even know if he has a wife or girlfriend.

Tabby arrived at the diner at the height of supper hour. Monday night specials were the best of the week. Homemade Shepherd's Pie,

Fried Shrimp Basket, or Vegetarian Omelet were written on the blackboard just inside the door announcing the nightly specials. The board was more for the benefit of non-locals because the regulars had the nightly meal deals memorized.

She looked around for an open table, and there were none. There wasn't even an open stool at the counter. She heard the door opened behind her and without looking, stepped aside so whoever it was could enter.

"Man, is this what it's like during tourist season?"

Tabby turned, and her heart gave a little flutter as she realized who it was standing behind her.

"Truthfully, I don't know," Tabby offered, blushing scarlet. "I lived outside town limits and had a boyfriend I cooked for every night. I haven't been in here for supper in a while."

"Had a boyfriend?" Greg asked, smiling.

Tabby blushed again. "Yes, had a boyfriend."

Judy Montgomery, one of the owners of the diner, approached them.

"Tabby, I can have a table for you in a couple of minutes. Mr. Stone, it will be about fifteen more minutes or so before I can get you seated. I don't know why we are so busy tonight. Vacation doesn't begin until next week. This is crazy."

"I can share my table with Mr. Stone, that is, if he doesn't mind," Tabby offered quietly.

"Well, Mr. Stone?" Judy asked.

"I wish you all would call me Greg. I would love to share my table with Miss Moon," he said, flashing that gorgeous smile that made Tabby melt inside.

"I'll be right back to get you," Judy replied, rushing off to clear a now vacant table.

"Do you eat here a lot?" Tabby asked, making small talk.

"Almost every night because I'm not a very good cook. Flowers, I'm a whiz. Cooking, not so much," he answered, chuckling.

An awkward silence descended upon the pair. Tabby hadn't been on a real date in six years, and her mind went blank as she tried to start a reasonable conversation with Greg. Why had she been so stupid to invite him to sit with her? She wasn't thinking straight at all. The little butterflies inside her stomach had done the thinking for her.

"All set," Judy said, returning with menus in her hand. "This way, please."

Judy seated the couple in a back booth in the corner and then winked at Tabby as she handed them each a menu.

"Bea will be right with you. Enjoy."

"I don't know why she bothered giving me a menu," Tabby stated. "I always have the Shepherd's Pie if I am here on Monday night."

"It's that good?"

"You won't find any better anywhere else. Listen to me, I sound like a commercial."

Bea Jones walked up to the table with order pad in hand. She spotted Tabby, broke into a smile, and gave her a big hug.

"How's your new place, hon?" she asked.

"It's beautiful. I'm going to make a batch of Gram's jellies and give them out to the townspeople on Saturday as a thank you for all they have done for me."

"I'll be first in line. I really miss your gram's jellies. The diner always served them while she was alive and cooking." She leaned in close to the young woman. "Of course, The Mouth has already spread it around town that you'll be making them again from her recipes."

"The Mouth?" Greg quizzed.

"Tabby will explain it to you later. What are we going to have for supper?"

"I think we have both decided on the Shepherd's Pie," Greg stated.

"I'll have a mocha frappe with mine, please," Tabby requested.

"Sounds good to me. Make that two," Greg said, picking up the menus and handing them to Bea.

Bea headed off to the kitchen to place their order.

"She is such a nice lady. Bea waits on me almost every night that I eat here. She is always smiling," Greg admired.

"Bea is like a second mother to me. Remember Jen who was with me in your shop yesterday? Bea is her mother," Tabby explained.

"So tell me, who is The Mouth?"

"Gladys Twittle. She and her husband Donald own the Penny Poor Antique Shop in the middle of town. He is really nice, but Gladys is loud, pushy and a pain in the butt. She has to know everything going on in town and will do anything to be on top of the latest gossip. Her favorite spot is the first stool closest to the register at the Tilted Coffee Cup every morning."

"I think I have seen her there. Does she wear dresses covered in flowers? I guess I decided to set up business in a colorful town, haven't I?"

"Yes, she does, and you have no idea just how colorful," Tabby agreed, laughing.

"Tell me about your shop. What is it and when will it open?" Greg questioned.

"It's called Jellies, Jams, and Weddings. I am a certified wedding planner, but I needed something besides weddings to pull customers into my shop. I will be cooking and selling my gram's preserves and homemade biscuits. People love her recipes, and I am the only one she entrusted them with. It's quirky, but I think it will work well together."

"Sounds interesting. What kind of account did you want to set up at my shop?" Greg inquired.

"I need an open account that I can order flowers for my own use or send my clients to you for their flower needs. It should bring in extra business for your shop."

"Are you sure you want to do that? I heard Jen say that your flowers were better than mine," Greg teased.

"She's biased. What can I say?"

"Maybe we need to have a flower-off some night when the shop is closed. I don't do the wedding flowers. My arranger Margaret Cook does them."

"Somehow I don't think that would be a good idea. We don't want to upset Margaret. She might quit on you," Tabby frowned.

"True. Not a good idea, I guess," Greg admitted.

Bea came to the table with their drinks. A few minutes later she arrived with hot steaming plates and set them on the table.

"Enjoy," she said, walking to another table to deliver their bill.

Jellies, Jams, and Bodies

"Enough with business talk. Tell me something interesting about yourself, Tabby Moon."

"My favorite holiday is Halloween."

"Mine, too," Greg laughed. "What else?"

"I am an avid reader like you, and my favorite genre is mystery. My secret wish is to someday solve a real mystery. My mother says I am too nosy. I'm not nosy, I just pay attention to things going on around me, that's all."

"I love mysteries, too. My aunt is a detective in Larsen. Sometimes when she calls me, we throw ideas back and forth. She says I have fresh eyes and can see things that she doesn't."

"Maybe we should team up together and find a mystery to solve," Tabby declared, blushing after thinking about what she had just said.

"I think that is an excellent idea," Greg said, flashing that million-watt smile.

In the middle of their supper, Gladys and Donald Twittle were seated in the booth next to Tabby and Greg. Bea walked to their table frowning. She leaned in and whispered something to Tabby, then walked away.

"What was that about?" Greg whispered.

Tabby leaned in close and beckoned him to move in closer.

"The Mouth saw us sitting here and requested that they be seated next to us. She smells new gossip to spread around at the coffee shop in the morning. Gladys wants to be close enough to hear what we are saying," Tabby whispered.

"Want to have some fun?" he asked, winking. "Follow my lead."

Tabby nodded.

"We won't tell your mother a thing," Greg suggested, in a voice a little louder than normal.

"I don't know," Tabby stuttered.

"We'll elope now and let your mother plan the big wedding she wants to at some point later on."

The young couple heard a spoon drop at the next table. Tabby put her hand to her mouth to stop the laughter that threatened to burst out of her. Greg signaled her to keep the conversation going now that they were sure Gladys was listening.

"I suppose we could do that. Do you think we can sneak off this weekend? Can you get someone to cover the flower shop for you? I'm off from the cable company on Saturday and Sunday."

"I'm sure I can. Where do you want to get married?" Greg questioned, stifling a laugh as out of the corner of his eye he could see Gladys' ear edging around the booth wall.

I think a private ceremony at Fuller's Point would be beautiful. What do you think?"

"Did you hear that, Donald? They're going to secretly get married," Gladys exclaimed with glee.

"No, I didn't hear it. I don't make it a habit to listen to other people's conversations and neither should you," her husband chastised. "No wonder people call you The Mouth."

Tabby and Greg almost fell out of the booth, laughing. Since both of them had finished their dinner and were ready to go, they signaled Bea for the bill. As they got up to leave, Gladys couldn't worm her way back into her own booth fast enough. She hit her tea and spilled it all over herself.

"Mrs. Twittle, I didn't know you were here. Are you okay? Was the tea hot?" Tabby commiserated, attempting a fake smile.

"No, I'm fine, thank you," she answered curtly, not bothering to look up.

"Okay, well, have a good night," Tabby said, trying to keep a straight face.

Greg grabbed hold of Tabby's hand. He leaned in but still talked loud enough for Gladys to hear him.

"I hope she didn't hear what we were talking about," he whispered as they walked to the register.

Bea met them at the counter. They told her about the prank they pulled on Gladys. Greg asked the waitress to play dumb if the gossip queen asked her any questions and she quickly agreed. They walked outside, turned the corner, and fell into fits of laughter.

"Do you think we did enough damage to the town gossip for one week?" Greg spit out between laughs, leaning against the diner wall.

"I can't wait to tell townspeople I don't know what they're talking about when they come to me for verification. That was classic, Mr. Stone."

"We make a pretty good team," Greg affirmed as he looked into her eyes.

"I guess we do," Tabby agreed, feeling hot all over.

"Come on, I'll walk you home. You can explain to me on the way what all the town's people did for you and why."

They walked down Main Street toward Tabby's place. She told him about the break-up with Finn and then the next night how her place was trashed. The police thought Finn had done it, but he didn't since he had an airtight alibi. She told him about the pickle jar and how the locals had donated money for her to get a fresh start.

"I like this town better by the minute. Keep your ears open for me. I need to find a place to live so I can stay here and not travel to Larsen every night. I like small-town living versus city living."

"I'll see what I can find out for you. We're here. That's my place across the street. I live over the Baseball Card Shop."

As they crossed the street, a flashlight beam could be seen moving toward the back room of the dark card shop.

"Did you see that?" Tabby questioned, not giving him time to answer. "Come on."

Tabby took off in a run with Greg close behind. They ran into the rear parking lot behind the building. They saw a dark figure haul himself over the back fence and take off. There was no use in chasing him.

The back door to the card shop was open. Tabby stepped through the door, calling Mr. Pierce's name. She found the light switch in the backroom. A very familiar scene met her eyes when the lights flared on. The shop had been trashed just like her apartment. Tabby began to shake as she stared in horror at the damage that surrounded her.

"Mr. Pierce, are you here?" Tabby finally yelled, composing herself.

No answer.

They inched their way into the main shop and discovered that it had been vandalized just like the backroom. The cellar door was standing wide open. Greg walked over to the top of the stairs.

"Mr. Pierce, are you down there? Tabby, do you know where the light switch is for the cellar?"

She stepped in front of Greg and reached for the string that would light up the area. Laying at the bottom of the stairs was a lifeless body—a body that was covered in blood.

7

"Call the authorities," Greg ordered as he flew down the stairs.

Tabby made the call as she followed Greg down into the cellar. Tabby reached down and tentatively felt for a pulse. There was none.

"The sheriff said he would be here in less than five minutes."

"Is it Mr. Pierce?" he asked.

"Yes, it is. The sheriff said not to touch anything."

"It's not going to be hard to figure out what the murder weapon was," Greg observed, pointing to a bloody baseball bat laying in the corner of the cellar.

"I guess not," Tabby agreed.

"Let's wait upstairs," Greg suggested.

Sheriff Puckett and his deputies arrived, blocking off the front of the store with their cars. As Tabby let them in the front door, she noticed that a crowd was gathering in front of the shop.

"Where is he?" the sheriff asked.

"He's at the bottom of the stairs," Greg responded.

"You can't stay away from trouble, can you? It always seems to find you, Tabitha Moon," Puckett said, shaking his head. "Stay up here."

The three men descended into the cellar as Tabby and Greg remained at the top of the stairs.

"Is this exactly how you found everything?" Deputy Small yelled from the cellar.

"We didn't touch anything except to feel for a pulse on his neck," Tabby stated.

Sheriff Puckett returned from the cellar and walked around upstairs surveying the area. He headed to the rear room where he checked the back door and found it had been jimmied.

"The victim must have surprised whoever was in here. There's blood on the stairs suggesting he was attacked up here and fell to the bottom."

"We saw the person run through the back parking lot and jump the fence," Greg informed them. "He was dressed all in black."

"And you would be?"

"Greg Stone, sir."

"The owner of the new flower shop in town?"

"Yes, sir."

"Nice to meet you," the sheriff said, sticking out his hand. "How did you get mixed up with our town sleuth?"

"Give me a break," Tabby stuttered.

"We shared a table at the crowded diner," Greg answered, smiling at Tabby.

"You say you saw the guy?"

"We didn't see who it was, but we saw him hop the back fence with no problem at all."

"What are you thinking, Tabby? I can see the wheels turning," the sheriff inquired.

"Twice I have witnessed Mr. Pierce and Larry Fink having a heated argument. I don't think Mr. Pierce knew anyone else in town except myself, Fink and Richard Wells."

"He knows me," the sheriff confirmed. "I had to pay him a visit after Richard came to see me in a huff. He claimed Fink was stealing from him. I started to check in with the renters to see what Fink was charging them versus what Richard said he should have been charging them."

"Do you know if Fink was ripping people off?"

"He sure was. Anywhere from one hundred to five hundred dollars per property. When I talked to Richard again and told him what I found out, he wanted Fink arrested on the spot."

"What did you tell him?" Tabby inquired.

"I told Richard I couldn't arrest the man on word of mouth evidence. I needed documentation of the facts he was claiming. I had to have the original leases that were in Fink's possession. He told me he'd get the proof I needed."

"How long ago was that before Mr. Wells disappeared?" Tabby questioned.

"Mr. Wells has disappeared?" Greg asked.

"It was the day of the public scream fest in the center of town. Yes, Richard is gone, and no one knows what happened to him," Sheriff Puckett informed him, answering both questions. "We have been trying to find him but haven't been able to come up with a clue as to what happened to him."

"It seems Larry Fink is right in the middle of everything happening in this quiet little town," Greg observed.

"I'm getting the same feeling, and we are watching him," the sheriff agreed. "If you two can't think of anything else, I need you to leave. We have a lot to do to process the scene. There hasn't been a murder here in over forty years. I almost have to pull out the manual to remember what has to be done."

The sheriff disappeared down the cellar stairs.

"Greg let's separate and mingle. I want to hear what is being said in the crowd, especially by Larry Fink if he's out there," Tabby suggested. "Do you know what Fink looks like?"

"I certainly do, I have to pay him my rent at the first of every month," Greg responded.

They slipped out the back, made their way out front and blended in with the crowd. Tabby situated herself within a couple of feet of Gladys. Greg came out of the alley on the other side of the building. He walked nonchalantly down the street and then stopped on the sidewalk right next to Larry Fink.

"What's going on?" Greg inquired.

"Gladys Twittle says there is someone dead inside the baseball shop," Fink replied.

"Someone's dead?" Greg asked, playing stupid. "The shop isn't even open yet."

"Yeah. I assume that it is probably the shop owner since no one else should be in there this time of night," Fink answered, looking around.

"Can you see the body?" Greg probed.

"No, I think it is down in the cellar. You can't see it through the windows," Fink stated.

"Down in the cellar, huh?"

Fink suddenly realized he had said too much. He turned and hurried to his office across the street. Greg walked over to where Tabby was standing. Gladys was telling everyone around her about the procedures the police should be following in the event of a murder. People were mesmerized and hanging on to every word she was saying. Trying her best to keep a straight face, Tabby spoke up.

"How do you know it was a murder?" she asked.

"Well, ah, I don't. I'm assuming…" Gladys stuttered.

"You know what they say about assuming something," Tabby stated, walking away to the sound of Gladys' husband chuckling under his breath.

Tabby and Greg strolled off together. They could hear Gladys as she fell off the topic of murder to the two of them and the so-called elopement plans she had listened in on at the diner. She had been shut down by Tabby on the murder topic, but that didn't stop The Mouth. This topic was much juicier, and people forgot all about the dead body in the shop when it came to gossip about one of their own. The young couple sat on the back stairs to Tabby's apartment and fell against each other laughing. Gladys had fallen for their story, hook, line, and sinker.

"My mom is not going to be happy when Gladys' story reaches her tomorrow," Tabby choked out in between her laughter. "What did Fink have to say?"

"He had deduced that since you couldn't see the body through the front windows on the main floor, the body must be in the cellar. I don't think he realized what he had said until after he said it. When I started asking him more questions, he got nervous and darted to his office for cover."

"Tabby! Where are you? Are you okay?" a high-pitched woman's voice questioned.

"Mom, I'm okay. I'm over here near the stairs," Tabby responded.

Samantha came out of the shadows, holding her chest where her heart was beating double time. Greg stood up.

"I saw the police cars roar down the street and saw the crowd standing around. I knew something bad had happened. It has, hasn't it? Something horrible has occurred!" her mother demanded to know.

"Mr. Pierce was murdered in his shop."

Samantha leaned forward and whispered to her daughter.

"Who's he?"

"Mom, this is Greg Stone. He owns the new flower shop that you've wanted me to visit."

"Nice to meet you," Greg stated.

"Did you meet each other at the shop?"

"Yes, we did. And we discovered we have the same taste in fountains," Greg answered with a potent smile.

"Not the frog fountain?" her mom asked in horror. "You're the phone bidder?"

"Guilty as charged."

"Well Tabitha, at least you can go visit the fountain now that you know where it is," her mom suggested, intuitively playing matchmaker.

"We have something we need to warn you about," Tabby said, looking sideways at Greg. "You might hear something around town tomorrow about Greg and me. It's not true."

"Tabitha Moon, what did you do?"

"We were sharing a booth at the diner because it was so crowded. Gladys asked to be seated next to us so she could overhear what we were saying. We kind of pulled a prank on her. We fed her a story that wasn't in any way true but made her think it was."

"Anyone standing out front of the baseball shop tonight has already heard the story from Gladys," Greg admitted.

"What did you let her overhear?"

"We said we were eloping this weekend and not telling you about our plans. We even discussed the fact that you wanted a large wedding. We agreed we would have one later so you would be happy. She almost fell out of her booth trying to listen to what we were saying."

"Tabitha Flower Moon, that's terrible. Funny, but terrible," her mother said, snickering. "And she fell for the whole thing, that's even funnier. She was in the coffee shop last weekend talking about you and Finn breaking up. How can she be that gullible?"

"I'm sure we will be the talk of the coffee shop tomorrow morning," Greg stated, laughing. "Flower?"

"Yes, that's my middle name," Tabby affirmed, rolling her eyes.

"Well Miss Tabitha Flower Moon, it's time for me to say goodnight," Greg said. "Six o'clock in the morning arrives mighty early. I have to be there for my flower delivery. Perhaps we can manage to *bump into* each other again for supper sometime?"

"Yes, I think that can be arranged," Tabby replied, feeling hot all over. "I need someone to bounce my ideas off to figure out what is going on in our quiet little town."

"I was hoping to be a date, not a sounding board," Greg frowned in response.

"I'm sorry, let me rephrase that. I would love to go on a date with you, Mr. Greg Stone."

"Really? How about Friday night?"

"That would be fine," Tabby agreed, her heart dancing a little flutter.

"Nice to meet you, Mrs. Moon."

"It's Ms., but you can call me Samantha."

"See you Friday night. Remember, play dumb if anyone asks you about our marriage plans," Greg insisted, laughing as he walked off.

They watched him disappear into the dark.

"He's cute," Samantha observed. "He definitely seems interested in you."

"Mom, we just met. He is really nice though. We both like a lot of the same things. He even paid for my supper tonight. That's more than Finn did in six years."

"I told you he was a loser," her mom insisted.

"I got the message, okay?" Tabby grumbled.

"It looks like the police are going to be here for a while. Now that I know you are okay, I am going to head home. You should go upstairs and stay out of the sheriff's way," Samantha admonished.

"I'm going upstairs, but it doesn't mean I can't watch out the front window," Tabby said, dodging a swat from her mother. "You know what I just thought of though?"

"What?"

"With Mr. Pierce dead, I wonder if he has any family that will take over the store and open it? If not, I may be able to get in there early and open for the summer season."

"His body's not even cold, and you want his store. Tabitha Moon, I did not raise you that way."

"I'm just saying… you're right. Thinking that way would make me a suspect. I killed him for his store. Good thing I have a solid alibi for tonight," Tabby said, thinking out loud.

"Go upstairs," her mom ordered. "Goodnight."

"Night, Mom. I love you."

Tabby sat in her new recliner watching the bustle outside. The coroner's van arrived and removed Mr. Pierce's body. As she watched, she noticed someone else was watching, too. Across the street in the second-floor window, Larry Fink was sitting, staring out the window. He wasn't smart enough to sit in the dark like Tabby was. The light on in the room behind him made it easy to identify him. The sheriff and the deputies left a few minutes after the coroner did. Fink shut off the light and disappeared for the night.

Tabby sat in the dark thinking. What if the killer did not find what he was looking for? What if he came back to search the upstairs? Was she safe staying in her apartment? To make matters worse, Mr. Pierce died a sudden and violent death. What if his ghost decided to stay in Tabby's shop?

Pull yourself together, woman.

Setting a cup of hot apple cinnamon tea down on her coffee table, Tabby opened her laptop and searched the name 'Larry Fink.' Then she searched for Lawrence Fink. There were seventeen possible matches.

Eleven had pictures, so Tabby could rule those out. The other six were all in the Midwest or on the West coast. There was no Larry or Lawrence Fink on the East coast.

Interesting...

She shut down the computer.

Saturday, I will pay a visit to Mr. Fink's office. I'll go on the pretense of finding out if the baseball shop will open or not. If he's not there, I can poke around. I will also ask him about who we pay rent to with Mr. Wells gone. I'll push the fact that Mr. Wells told me Larry Fink would not be in charge of rentals anymore. Let's see what kind of reaction that gets.

The rest of the week was quiet in the small town. Tabby left work an hour early on Friday to get ready for her date. She wasn't sure what to wear since Greg hadn't said where they were going or what they would be doing. Black slacks, a purple blouse, and black flats finally won out. She applied her makeup with a light hand and added a touch of clear lip gloss. She was dressed up enough for dinner or had pants on if they did something a little more athletic like bowling.

Greg arrived at six o'clock, right on time. Since Finn had never been on time Tabby realized that she was going to have to adjust her expectations. He whistled when she opened the door. Her breathing came a little faster. She looked downwards so he wouldn't see her blushing.

"You look gorgeous tonight!" Greg smiled. "Are you ready to go?"

"I wasn't sure how to dress. Where are we going?"

"It's a surprise. You are dressed just fine."

Twenty minutes later they pulled up in front of The Harbor Side Restaurant in Larsen. Carriage lights lit up the sidewalk. A uniformed parking attendant opened the door for Tabby as she stepped out and waited for Greg.

"Are you ready for dinner?" he asked, extending his arm for her to hold.

"I have always wanted to eat here. Everyone says the food is to die for. Oh, I am so sorry- poor choice of words," Tabby stated with a small laugh.

They entered the foyer. Beautiful stained-glass windows surrounded black wrought-iron benches where people could sit and wait for their tables. The couple walked up to the reservation desk.

"May I help you?"

"We have a reservation under the name of Stone for seven o'clock," Greg answered.

"It will be just a few minutes. Please take a seat in the waiting area. A waitress will be right with you if you would like to order a cocktail while you wait."

They had just seated themselves when a smiling waitress arrived to take their drink order. Tabby ordered a glass of wine and Greg ordered a beer. The couple chatted for about twenty minutes. The hostess came to get them, and they were seated next to a window overlooking the water.

"It is so beautiful," Tabby said, looking out at the harbor lights. "Have you eaten here before?"

"Once. I came here with my mom before she died."

"I'm so sorry. I didn't know," Tabby sympathized.

"You don't have to be sorry. My dad died when I was ten. It was just my mom and me growing up. She's the reason I love flowers like I do. We were always in her gardens on a sunny day. Every day she would stand in the middle of the garden and yell, "Smells so fine." That's where the shop name came from. She died of cancer four years ago. The only thing I regret is she never got to see my shop. I'm sure she would have loved it."

"You have no other family?"

"I have one uncle in California and a couple of cousins that I haven't talked to since my mom's funeral," Greg replied.

"Kind of sounds like me. It's always been just me and my mom, the town hippie. I don't even know who my dad was, and we have no other close relatives."

The waitress arrived at their table ready to take their order.

"Have whatever you want," Greg offered.

"Are you sure? I have quite an appetite," Tabby responded.

"Good. I hate women that are afraid to eat in front of men. Order away," Greg said, picking up his beer.

Tabby decided to order with gusto, so she chose the surf and turf right off the Specials Board. She started with a salad topped with Russian dressing. Greg selected the fisherman's platter with onion rings. Instead of salad, he ordered French onion soup. As they attacked the appetizers, Greg requested another round of drinks.

They talked about their childhoods, schooling, and what hobbies they shared. They had so much in common, much more than Tabby could have ever imagined. They discussed Tabby losing the frog fountain to Greg and how mad she was at the phone bidder at the time. Then the conversation turned to holidays. Tabby had enough wine that she felt comfortable talking to Greg and telling him her feelings.

"Someday I'm going to have a Halloween wedding. Finn and I talked about it, but he backed out."

"What do you mean he backed out?"

"We had been going together for about four years. He didn't want to commit, but I insisted on it. I planned a beautiful Halloween wedding. The invitations went out, and two months before the wedding he backed out. I should have dumped his sorry butt then, but I didn't. He talked me into giving him more time, and I fell for it. What a fool I was."

"I'm sorry, Tabby. He's the fool for letting you get away," Greg insisted, taking her hand gently in his.

Tabby didn't pull away as she realized that she liked the feel of Greg holding her hand. In the short time that she had known him, she felt closer to him than she had with Finn for six years. She stared at Greg realizing that he was great looking, caring, and funny. He made her insides melt when he came near her. She admitted to herself that she could fall in love with Greg Stone very easily.

Duh, can you say rushing things?

Her head was spinning, and she didn't know if it was from the wine or the way he paid attention to her, or the combination of both. He made her feel like she was special like she was the only person in his world right now.

"All right, do I have something stuck between my teeth?"

"No, why?" Tabby asked.

"You're sitting there staring at me and not hearing a word I am saying," Greg answered, smiling. "Am I boring you?"

"No, not at all. I was just thinking how easy it is to talk to you," Tabby blurted out before she could catch herself. She felt the warm crimson rise up in her chest to cover her face.

"I was thinking the same thing about you earlier," Greg said, picking up his fork.

"You were?"

"Yes, I was. Don't you worry, Tabitha Moon. Someday you will have that fancy Halloween wedding, just you wait and see," he predicted.

The waitress showed up at their table to check on them and to ask if they wanted any coffee or dessert.

"How about we share a dessert?" Greg suggested with a saucy wink.

Tabby nodded in agreement.

"Two coffees and a strawberry shortcake with extra whipped cream and two spoons, please," Greg requested as he handed the waitress his empty plate.

"I love strawberry shortcake. It's my favorite," Tabby said, eyeing him suspiciously. "Did you already know that?"

"No, I ordered it because it's my favorite dessert. I was hoping you would like it, too."

When dessert was served, Greg swiped a finger full of whipped cream and dabbed it onto Tabby's nose. She tried to reciprocate, but her arms weren't long enough when Greg sat back in his chair, so she ate the blob of whipped cream instead.

"I am going to fire up the frog fountain for the first time tomorrow. Want to come watch?" Greg asked.

"What time?"

"Around ten. I'm serving refreshments for the official start of the frogs playing in the water. I have named them all, you know."

"You named all the frogs?"

"Yes. When you come to see the fountain tomorrow, I will introduce you to them."

"You are too funny. Larry Fink's office opens at nine. I am hoping his secretary will be the only one there and if I can keep her busy, I could nose around a bit. I can be at your shop by ten. I'd like to see *my* fountain working," Tabby agreed, laughing.

"What are you looking for at Fink's office?"

"Anything to see why he was fighting with Mr. Pierce and if he had anything to do with Mr. Well's disappearance. All the original leases are somewhere in the office, too. I have a gut feeling that all of this involves the drive-in on the edge of town."

"Why do you think that?"

"The night that Richard Wells disappeared there was a set of blueprints for the drive-in on his dining room table. I thought that was kind of odd because he doesn't own that property. It seemed to stand out from all the other documents on his table that dealt with the property he *did* own. I can't shake the idea that he had it for a specific reason, although I can't seem to figure out what that reason might be."

"Maybe he was going to buy it?" Greg suggested.

"No, he's selling off all his properties to retire to Florida. Besides, a drive-in would be too much for him to handle at his age. No, there is some other reason he had that blueprint which somehow managed to end up inside my purse."

"You *stole* it from the old man's house?" Greg asked surprised.

"No, I borrowed it with the intent to give it back when I find him," Tabby countered with a smile. "There's a difference."

"Where do you think he is?"

"Personally, I think Fink has him stashed somewhere."

"Why do you think that?"

"Because Richard was going to take all his rental business away from him. I think Fink is going to get all the money he can and take off with it. To do that, he had to keep Richard quiet and out of the way. Rent is due next week, and nothing has been said about returning the rent amounts to what was supposed to be charged according to the leases."

"If Larry Fink is that dangerous that you think he has Wells, you had better take care. I don't want you disappearing before I have a chance at a second date," Greg advised with a sexy smile.

"I'll be careful, I promise. After I leave your shop tomorrow, I am

Jellies, Jams, and Bodies

going out to the drive-in to look around. The Swansons usually have everything up and running by Memorial Day Weekend."

"Why don't you wait until two o'clock and I'll go with you? Sally closes on Saturdays. It's my only afternoon off."

"Deal. I'll drive so you can take it easy on your only day off," Tabby quipped, joking with him.

The waitress appeared and delivered their bill to them with a flourish.

"Dutch?" Tabby inquired.

"Not on your life. I asked you out on a date. You will never pay for anything when you are out with me, Miss Moon," Greg responded, assisting her up from her seat.

The ride home was short, and Tabby hated to see the night end. Greg parked on Main Street and came around to open the car door for her like a true gentleman. He took her hand as they walked to the back stairs to Tabby's apartment. She shivered as Greg took her hand.

"Are you okay?" he asked, noticing the shiver.

"I'm just perfect," Tabby assured him, smiling.

He walked her up the stairs and waited for her to find the keys in her purse. She opened the door and turned to thank him. He gently kissed her on the lips and said good night. Tabby watched him walk down the stairs as the worst case of butterflies she had ever had made her full stomach dance a polka. As Greg's car roared to life, Tabby stepped inside, locking and dead-bolting the door behind her.

She brushed her teeth, changed into her customary sweats and a tee then crawled into bed pondering the last few hours. She glanced over at the lighted cell phone charging on the nightstand next to the bed. Tabby had never believed in love at first sight, but she was beginning to change her mind because of Greg. She was looking forward to tomorrow. As her eyes drifted closed her mind replayed all the evening's events, and she smiled softly in her sleep.

Tabby was up early the next morning. She did more searching on the web for Fink and his companies. Two cups of coffee later, and no new information on her suspect, she dressed in jeans and sneakers for the day's business. Standing in her front window, she watched Fink leave his realty company. Noticing that he didn't lock the door, she watched him walk up the street.

This is my chance. I can distract the secretary and look around.

She grabbed her purse and cell phone and ran down the back stairs. Crossing the street, keeping her eyes open for Fink's return, she entered the realty office. The secretary was sitting at the front desk.

"Can I help you?" the secretary offered.

"Yes, you can. Mr. Wells was supposed to have a lease drawn up for my new apartment rental above the baseball card shop. My rent is coming due very shortly, and I don't even know what I am supposed to be paying. He said somewhere around four hundred a month," Tabby answered.

"I can check the files downstairs to see if there is a lease for you," the secretary informed her as she stood up from her chair.

"I also need to talk to someone about the baseball card shop and whether it will be opening now."

"I haven't heard anything on the future of the shop yet. The only one who will have that answer is Mr. Fink. Let me go check on that lease for you."

"Thank you."

As soon as the lady disappeared down the stairs, Tabby made a break for Fink's office. She rummaged through the papers on top of the desk but didn't find anything pertinent. A small table stood in the corner of the room with family pictures arranged in small groups.

At least he loves his family.

The table behind his desk held something very interesting. There was an identical copy to the drive-in blueprint that Tabby had. Only this one was written over in red ink showing new land boundaries and a developer's name in some of the new spaces marked off on the blueprint. Tabby hurriedly rolled it up and stuck it down inside the cavern of her purse. She hurried back to the spot where she had been standing when Larry Fink came whistling through the front door.

"What are you doing here? Where is Stella?" Fink questioned nervously.

"She went to check to see if my new lease is ready for the apartment,"

Tabby answered innocently. "Rent is coming up, and I don't know what I am supposed to be paying. Mr. Wells said about four hundred a month, but I haven't seen a lease."

"There is no lease drawn up yet. If Richard told you four hundred, then pay four hundred. Is there anything else?"

"Yes. I need to know what is happening with the baseball card shop. Is it opening or is it going to be cleaned out by family? Your secretary said you were the only one who would know what was going on."

"Mr. Pierce has no family or heirs that I am aware of. No one else was listed on the lease. If you want to do the work yourself and put his store stock down in the cellar, you can have the building now. I really don't care one way, or another" Fink answered brusquely. "NOW, is there anything else?"

"When can I get the keys?" Tabby asked, pushing to get them so she could check out the equipment that Mr. Pierce left behind in his shop and because the door between the two floors had been locked.

"If I give you the keys now, will you go away and leave me alone?" Fink groused.

"Gladly," Tabby agreed.

The realtor stalked to his office, picked up a set of keys and rudely threw them at her.

"Personally, the store isn't my concern anymore. You can move in tomorrow for all I care. I don't know what the rent will be, and I won't be here long enough to collect it. Now get the heck out of my office," Fink demanded as he fidgeted anxiously with his tie.

"If I won't be paying my rent to you, do you know when Mr. Wells will be back so that I can to get the information from him?" Tabby challenged, pushing him some more.

"I don't know where Wells went, and I don't care about that either. You know he was taking all his business away from me, so don't play stupid. I hope he rots where ever he is," Fink yelled. "Get out, now!"

Tabby hurried out of the office. She could feel Larry Fink's cold eyes boring a hole in her back as she walked up the street. She turned around, found him still standing in the door watching her, so she smiled and waved. He glared at her and disappeared into the realty building.

It was just before ten when she reached the flower shop. It was busier than usual as people had come from miles around just to view the official start-up of the frog fountain. It didn't hurt that Greg was giving away free food and drinks either. Tabby sauntered in, and Greg broke away from the crowd to come take her hand. She held up the set of keys Fink had given her to the shop.

"What do you have there?" Greg inquired.

"Keys to the baseball shop. It's now mine," Tabby declared excitedly.

"Seriously?"

"I'll tell you everything when we go to the drive-in later. Right now, I want to see *my* fountain working."

"I was waiting for you to get here. Let's go turn this baby on. Then, I'll tell you all the frogs' names," he said with a smile.

They walked together to the back of the shop, and Greg stepped forward to thank everyone who had shown up for the big event. He gave a short explanation as to the history of the fountain, teasing Tabby that they had unknowingly battled each other for ownership of it and he had won. He invited everyone to come with their morning coffee and sit by the fountain to start their day.

Gladys Twittle and Mrs. Ryan were standing at the back of the store, their plates overflowing with food. They were whispering back and forth and smiling. Tabby gave them a little wave knowing they were talking about the supposed elopement. Greg climbed behind the fountain, and a few seconds later, the water was cascading down its steps. As the water splashed over the frogs, it looked like they were playing in the flowing water.

Tabby's spirit drooped a little thinking this could have been in the center of her new shop. Her face must have been sobered with a frown as Greg came over to her when he came back from behind the fountain. He went to her and put his arm around her shoulder.

"I'm sorry you are so sad," he whispered in her ear.

"It's okay. It was the initial shock of seeing the fountain working. I do love the way you have filled the bottom level with water lily plants. I guess it does have a better home here with flowers rather than with jellies and jams. I hope you understand I will be here visiting the frogs quite often," Tabby said, smiling, taking hold of the hand that was draped on her shoulder.

"Just the frogs? What about me?"

"All right, I guess I can visit with you at the same time," Tabby replied with a hint of humor in her voice.

Gladys and Mrs. Ryan shuffled past them as they made their second trip to the food table.

"See, I told you," Gladys whispered to her fellow gossiper.

"I never would have believed it," Mrs. Ryan answered in disbelief.

"Believed what?" Tabby asked as the two women passed by.

"Oh, nothing," Gladys retorted. "Nothing at all."

The two women stood at the food table giggling like teenagers that knew a secret. Greg was watching them, thoroughly amused at how gullible they were. He decided to give them a little more to talk about.

"Are you ready to go, honey?" he asked, quite loudly.

Tabby looked over at the food table and realized what he was doing. She elbowed him in the stomach.

"You are so bad," she whispered to Greg.

"I know, but it's so much fun," he muttered under his breath so only she could hear.

"They're going to think we're eloping when we are only driving down to the drive-in. Won't they be shocked when we return in a couple of hours?" Tabby replied.

"Watch their faces," Greg instructed as Margaret came from the back room.

"Are you sure you can handle things while I am away?" Greg questioned, yelling across the room to Margaret who had stopped at the register.

"It's good. I can handle things here. Go and enjoy your time off," Margaret answered.

"Okay then, we are off and running," Greg replied, grabbing a bridal bouquet out of the display refrigerator.

No one noticed what he did except for the two women at the food table who almost dropped their plates. They hurried past the young couple and headed straight for the Tilted Coffee Cup across the street.

This would be the hottest gossip they had to report in weeks. As soon as they were out of sight, Greg put the bridal bouquet back on display.

"You are rotten," Tabby confirmed, laughing hysterically. "Did you see their faces?"

"Let's get out of here before they come back," he said, grabbing her hand and pulling her out of the shop.

They strolled down Main Street, hand in hand, not realizing people were staring at them. Without thinking, they were feeding the gossip that would soon be all over town. Since Tabby's car was parked out in the back lot, they headed in that direction. They climbed into the car and drove back up Main Street heading to the drive-in which was located just outside of town to the north. When the car passed the coffee shop, people were staring out the window alongside Gladys and Mrs. Ryan. They were probably saying "I told you so" to anyone who would care to listen.

Tabby expected people to be flitting around the property. The weeks prior to opening night was spent cleaning and getting the place ready for the summer season. As the couple pulled up to the ticket booth, they realized the chains were still in place closing off the parking area in front of the tall screen. The place was deserted.

"What the heck is going on?" Tabby inquired, as she exited the car. "Where is everyone?"

"It isn't open during the day," Greg replied as he stood up.

"Look over there," Tabby said, pointing to the office.

Taped to the front window was a sign that said the drive-in was permanently closed. As Tabby was reading the sign, she heard a noise coming from the back of the ticket booth.

"What..." Greg started to say.

"Shhh," Tabby requested, putting her finger to her lips.

She pointed to the back of the booth and motioned for Greg to follow her. They turned the corner and heard the noise again. A cardboard box was pushed up against the back door of the booth. It moved, and faint noises could be heard coming from inside the box.

"Let me check it" Greg insisted, waving Tabby away from the box. He picked it up and opened it.

8

"Unbelievable," Greg said, shaking his head.

"What?" Tabby asked.

"Come look."

Greg gently opened the box again. Tabby walked forward and peered in. Two small kittens, one orange and white and one all white, were trying desperately to get out of the box. They started meowing very loudly. Tabby picked them up and snuggled them into her fleece vest.

"Who would do something like this?" Greg wondered.

"Someone who figured the place would be opening and people would be here working this week," Tabby replied. "I wonder how long they've been here?"

"There's no food in the box or anything for them to sleep on. They're probably hungry," Greg said, taking the white one, rubbing him under the chin.

"You two lucked out. I was going to get an older cat at the shelter next Saturday. I guess I now have two kittens for my new apartment. Greg, do you mind if we head back to town? I want to go to Mac's and get some cat supplies before the store closes. I'll come back tomorrow and poke around."

They gently placed the kittens back in the box and Tabby set the box in Greg's lap once he hooked up his seatbelt. The ride back to town was a noisy one since the kittens were not happy about being back in the box. Tabby pulled the car into the side parking lot of Mac's supermarket. She took the box from Greg so he could get out of the car and then gently placed the carton in the back seat.

"I bet they are out and wandering around the car by the time we get out of the store," Greg remarked. "We'll have to check before we open the doors."

Tabby loaded up on all the kitten necessities: hard food, soft food, treats, toys, a litter box, and milk. While they waited in line, they discussed names for the kittens. They decided that the white kitten's name should be Ghost and the smaller orange one's obviously needed to be Marmalade.

Tabby decided that once she had the new shop set up downstairs, she would install a cat door on the door that led up to the apartment. That way the cats could come and go as they pleased and visit her while she was working in the shop. There would be no open food served in the shop so it would not be an issue with the Board of Health. Greg volunteered to install it for her.

They arrived at Tabby's apartment where Greg carted all the groceries upstairs, and Tabby followed with the box of howling fur.

"Nice place," Greg observed, setting the bags down in the kitchen.

"I really like it. It's not too big, but it's not small either. It's comfortable. The best part is that it's convenient to everything and I will be working right downstairs. Now that I can lease the shop early than I planned, I won't have to use the second bedroom as a storage area. I can actually set it up and use it as a second bedroom."

Tabby softly set the box on the floor, and she closed the door behind her.

"Are you ready?" she asked excitedly, as she opened the box to let the kittens out to roam.

Ghost took off heading for the bedroom and hid under the bed. Marmalade looked around and sat down, not moving away from the box.

"She's afraid," Greg determined, bending down to pick her up.

"Why don't you sit and hold her while I set up the litter box? Then I need to show you what I found today."

Tabby set up the new litter box in the bathroom and left the door open so the kittens could find the box while they were nosing around. She came down the hallway to see Greg snuggling the kitten and talking quietly to her. Marmalade had curled up on his shoulder.

"She likes you," Tabby said, kneeling next to the recliner.

"She's a sweetheart," Greg replied with a smile.

"I'm going to show her where the litter box is," Tabby asserted, taking the kitten off Greg's shoulder.

The kitten let out a loud meow. She didn't want to leave the spot where she felt protected and safe.

"I think she likes you better than me," Tabby pouted.

Tabby placed the kitten in the litter box and watched with pride as Marmalade did her business right away. She waddled out of the bathroom and spotted Ghost in the bedroom. Marmalade decided to go check out what her brother was doing.

The first plan that Tabby *borrowed* from Richard Well's cabin was in the spare room. She grabbed it along with the new one she had taken from Fink's office. She spread them both out on her kitchen table.

"Come look at these."

Greg compared the two blueprints. Richard Wells' print was the original one. The one from Fink's office had new boundary lines drawn, and the drive-in property looked like it had been divided into two separate properties. The smaller section created by the division had Fink's name on it. The larger had a development company's name printed across it.

"It looks like the drive-in has been sold, either by Fink or to Fink. He, in turn, divided the property and sold some of it off," Greg commented, pointing at each area he was referring to.

"No way. Peyton Swanson died, and he left the business to his wife, Marsha. I found out she died a couple of months ago, right after her husband. The property was left to Marsha's brother, Samuel Walters, in Portland. He's quite a bit younger than Marsha and was going to carry on the family business."

"Could he have sold the business to Fink after he inherited it?"

"Not even remotely possible. If Marsha thought for even a moment that Samuel would sell off the property, she wouldn't have left it to him," Tabby declared as her brows creased into a furrow of concentration. "He has children that the property could be left to when he retired."

"The big question is, how did Fink get his hands on the property?"

"That is what we have to find out. I think Richard Wells was looking into what was going on, too. He must have found something, and that's why he disappeared. Why else would he have had this blueprint at his cabin?"

"I'll write the recorded deeds down and check them out at the town hall on my way to work on Monday. I'll find out who's listed as the owner and the dates of the most recent filed deeds for the divided property. That should give us somewhere to start," Greg confirmed.

Marmalade had come out of the bedroom and was rubbing up against Greg's leg. He picked her up, and the purring started almost instantly.

"She seems to be more your cat than mine," Tabby observed with a frown.

"I was just the first one to pay attention to her. Here, you hold her and talk to her. I'm sure she'll love you just as much," he chuckled, handing the kitten to her.

Tabby took the kitten and snuggled her down into her arm. She talked softly to the kitten and rubbed her soft fur at the same time. Marmalade settled down and began to purr. She closed her eyes and went to sleep in Tabby's arms.

"See, she had to get to know your smell. Marmalade is going to be a real love bug."

"She does like me," Tabby said, smiling happily.

"I don't know about you, but I'm hungry. We didn't have lunch. The diner will probably be packed. Why don't we go to that little café just outside of town?"

"I love that place. It's still early enough that we can go eat and I can come back and type my resignation letter to Common Cable. I have a store to open now, and I want to get started as soon as possible. Luckily,

Jellies, Jams, and Bodies

I have already ordered all the items I need to start making my jellies and jams. My supplies should have been here by now. I will have to check the tracking to see where they are in route."

"I can't wait to taste this jelly that everyone claims is the ambrosia of the gods," Greg teased as he was walking toward the door.

"Gram's recipes are awesome. I need to expand the line of flavors, so I'm trying a new one on my own. It's called Blood Orange Jelly."

"Spooky. Shouldn't you save that one for Halloween?" Greg suggested.

"I suppose I could come up with a summertime jelly instead. We'll see," Tabby agreed,

putting Marmalade down on the floor.

She wandered off to go join her brother who was still hiding in the bedroom. Tabby made certain the door was closed tightly and locked, and they left.

The Outdoor Café was almost empty. On Saturday nights, the Whipper Will Diner had seafood specials which always drew in big crowds. It was nice not to have to fight for a table. The night was warm, so they asked the hostess if they could eat on the patio. She put them in the far corner so they could have some privacy. It was secluded, but at the same time, you could see the entire inside of the restaurant. They ordered cocktails and looked over their menus.

"When are you planning to open your shop?" Greg inquired.

"I'm going to shoot for some time in June," she replied.

"What's going to happen to all the baseball stuff?"

"Larry Fink said he didn't care what happened to it. I'm going to pack it up and put it downstairs in the cellar until I can talk to Mr. Wells about it."

Suddenly Tabby got very quiet as she bit her lip to prevent herself from tearing up. Growing up, this telltale sign would always alert her mother to the fact that she was upset. Sometimes Tabby would bite her lip so bad it would bleed.

"Thinking about Richard Wells?" Greg questioned, taking her hand in his.

"We need to find him. I have a feeling he's somewhere close, I just haven't figured out where yet. I hope he's okay. He's not a spring chicken, and I don't know how much his body can take. The sheriff keeps coming up with nothing but dead ends in all of his searching."

"We'll find him. If we figure out what is happening with the drive-in property, we can figure out where he is and who has him."

The waitress appeared to take their order. They both ordered a pulled pork sandwich with coleslaw. Tabby requested a second glass of wine and Greg opted for another beer.

The conversation came easy between them. When one topic ended, they slid seamlessly into the next one. A few times while they were talking, Greg took hold of Tabby's hand, and she would feel a slight tingle in her fingers where they touched.

"Does this qualify as a second date?" Greg asked, with a boyish grin.

"I think it does, Mr. Stone. Why, do you have something in mind?"

"I was wondering how many dates we had to have before I could call you my girlfriend," he said, looking in her eyes.

"We haven't even known each other for a week," Tabby protested. "Let's take this one day at a time, okay?"

"Okay. I know you just broke up with your last boyfriend, but I am a firm believer in love at first sight. My mom and dad got married after three months. Sometimes, you just know," he claimed, taking a sip of his beer.

Tabby looked at him like he had read her mind. She was thinking the same thing at the end of their first date.

"Give me the dessert menu, quick," Tabby demanded, putting her hand over her eyes and looking downward.

As Greg handed her the menu, he looked confused. One minute they were talking about love at first sight and the next, she was hiding behind a menu.

"What's going on?" he whispered.

"Larry Fink and some dark-haired woman were just seated in the dining room. I didn't want them to see me," Tabby answered. "Can you make out who the woman is that's with him?"

"I don't know, I can't see her. It's too bad we're not closer so we can hear what they're saying," Greg said, peering through the window at them.

As Fink was talking to his dinner guest, he looked over the top of his menu and spotted Greg staring through the window at him. He slammed the menu down and stood up. Bending over and saying something to the woman, they left in a hurry. The woman hid her face as they ran out the door.

"I'm going to follow them and see if I can figure out who she is," Tabby announced, jumping up and bolting for the front door.

Greg was close behind, but by the time they made it to the parking lot the car was pulling away and the passenger was ducking down so she couldn't be seen.

"Crap. I wonder who she is? No one in town has long black hair like that," Tabby commented.

The waitress had no idea what was going on as she stood by their table holding a tray full of food. When she saw them reenter the restaurant, she set their meals down relieved that they hadn't skipped on their tab.

"Sorry. We thought we knew those people who just left," Greg apologized.

"You mean Mr. Fink? He eats here all the time. I don't know who his lady friend was though. I have never seen her in here before tonight. They sure left in a hurry. No explanation, just up and gone," the waitress said, looking at the door. "At last, they didn't order anything before they ran off."

"Do you know Mr. Fink well?" Tabby inquired.

"No, he's pretty quiet when he's here. Great tipper, though," the waitress said, smiling. "I was sad to them leave. He would have been the best tip of the night."

"I'm sorry you missed out," Greg said.

"Oh, don't be sorry. It was nothing that you folks did. Do you need refills on your drinks?"

"Sure, but this time around would you bring us two of your biggest and best sweet iced teas," Greg requested with a smile.

"I feel so bad we chased her big tip away," Tabby said when the waitress left to get their drinks.

"We'll leave her a good tip," Greg promised. "At least we know where Fink eats every night. I don't know if he will come back now that we have seen him here."

"How did he get control of the drive-in property? Before I can even figure that out, it looks like he has sold some of it off to a developer. I wonder if it is the same developer that wanted to buy the Starling Apartments," Tabby pondered.

"Are you talking to yourself or to me?" Greg quizzed.

"I'm sorry. I talk to myself a lot. I'm not used to having someone around that can carry on an intelligent conversation, short of Jen."

"Are you saying your last boyfriend was two sandwiches short a picnic?" Greg chuckled, digging into his coleslaw.

"He wasn't stupid, but the only things he could talk about were himself or his things."

"His things?"

"He was a hoarder. When he filled up his own house, he tried to bring piles of stuff to my house. That was the last straw for me. I threw him and his junk out."

"I'm definitely not a hoarder. The only thing I do collect is books. My mom bought first editions. That's what got me started. I have a nice library in my house that holds my collection."

"I had a small collection of teddy bears that had been left to me by my gram, but whoever broke into my house destroyed them all. I do have a start for a new collection." She opened her purse and pulled one out. "Mr. Wells gave me this jelly bear to put in my new shop for good luck."

"He's cute."

"You have your own house?" Tabby asked. "In Larsen?"

"It was actually my gran's house. She and Gramps bought the house back in the forties, and I inherited it since I was the only family left on my mom's side. I also inherited my mom and dad's house, but I sold it. Gran's house is an old Victorian with lots of character. I even found a hidden tunnel in the basement."

"A tunnel? That's so cool."

"They say the house was on the Underground Railroad to Canada. I haven't found any proof of that yet, though."

"If you have such a great house, why do you want to move to Whipper Will Junction?"

"I would like to find a smaller house here, and I love the atmosphere of this town... it is so laid back. Plus, I really don't want to drive to and from Larsen in the snow come winter time. I will still hold on to gran's house. Maybe I will rent it out for a year or two and then sell it. I don't know yet."

"I can't blame you there. The roads here aren't the greatest during the winter. If it snows really bad, the roads may be closed for several days. Quite often Whipper Will Junction gets cut off from the outside world."

"I can't afford to be out of town and not be able to get to my store for Valentine's Day. That would be a disaster for my business. Please keep your ears open for any house or apartment that is for rent year-round," Greg requested.

"I'll check around for you," Tabby agreed, finishing her last bite of supper. "Do you know what this place is famous for?"

"I didn't know that a little place like this could be famous for anything. Tell me, what is it famous for?"

"It's massive strawberry shortcake," answered Tabby, smiling. "Want to split one?"

"You can't eat one by yourself?"

"They are huge. It's a two-person dessert."

Greg called the waitress over and ordered two coffees and one dessert.

"You know, I was thinking," Greg said. "When did Mr. Wells give you that bear?"

"He gave it to me on Saturday afternoon."

"Right before the break-in on Sunday? The same weekend?"

"Yes, now that you mention it."

"Did anyone see him give you the bear?"

"Larry Fink was watching us from his realty office."

"I think it was the bear that someone was looking for when they broke into your apartment. You haven't taken it out of your purse since then?"

"No, I have carried it with me to keep Mr. Wells close in my thoughts."

"May I see the bear, please?"

Greg was looking over the stuffed animal when their dessert and coffee arrived.

"I recognize that bear, I collect them. Which one did you get? Ah, strawberry jelly bear. They make those by hand in a little shop over in Milbridge. She has a whole line of different foods that the bears hold," their waitress said, putting down their order on the table.

"Do you know the name of the shop?" Tabby asked.

"Sure, it's the Bear Cottage. It's right next to The Milbridge First Commerce Bank. Enjoy your dessert."

Tabby was digging into the large strawberries while Greg looked over the bear. He found some stitches on the side of the bear that didn't look like they belonged there. He showed them to Tabby.

"If I'm careful, do you want me to open the stitches?" Greg inquired.

"Go ahead, let's see if your hunch is right."

Greg took out his pocket knife. He slowly and carefully sliced the stitches one at a time. He had the side of the bear opened about an inch and a half when something caught his eye. He reached into the stuffing and pulled out a key.

"What kind of key is that?" Tabby wondered. "Look on the back. There's a seven-seven-two engraved on it."

"That is what the intruder was looking for when your apartment got trashed. Didn't you say all your bears were ripped apart? This is why."

"I know where I saw the number on the key. It was on the back of Mr. Wells blueprint of the drive-in, along with the letters MFC."

"And where did the waitress say the bear store was near? Milbridge First Commerce Bank? MFC," Greg affirmed. "I believe this is a safety deposit box key."

"What could be so important in that box that Mr. Well's life would be put in jeopardy?"

Jellies, Jams, and Bodies

"I don't know, but we aren't Mr. Wells so we can't get in the box and find out either," Greg sighed.

"At least I know why my apartment was trashed. I have to call Sheriff Puckett and let him know what's going on," Tabby stated.

"If you do that, you'll have to tell him how you got the blueprint," Greg said, popping a strawberry in his mouth.

"You're right. Maybe it will be better to keep this between you and me for now," Tabby agreed. "Jen told me to get my place alarmed when the store opens. I think I need to do that now. If this key is that important to Fink, he may trash my new place."

"You need to keep this bear in your purse where he has been and don't flash him around. If Fink knows you are carrying it with you, you may end up like Mr. Wells—among the missing."

Tabby pulled a pack of gum out of her purse.

"You haven't finished dessert. What's with the gum?" Greg asked.

"Watch."

She pushed a small indent on the side of the gum package. The top slid open. Inside was a key. She added Mr. Wells key to the little drawer and slid it closed. She placed it in a zippered pocket in her purse alongside cough drops and breath mints.

"Very clever."

"My mom gave it to me so I would always have a spare car key with me. When I first started driving, I locked myself out of my car quite a few times. She got tired of bringing her key to bail me out. She had a spare made and gave me this little gum case so no one would know it was a key. The funny part is, since she gave me the spare key, I haven't locked myself out."

"We should sew up the bear again. If something happens and Fink does get to it, he'll take the bear and run. If it's open, he'll know the key is not there anymore," Greg suggested, finishing his coffee.

"I'll do it when I get home tonight," Tabby agreed, putting the bear back in her purse.

"I want you to be really careful. Fink probably thinks we are following him now that we saw him tonight. Don't go anywhere alone," Greg cautioned as he took hold of her hand.

"I won't go anywhere without you or Jen by my side," Tabby promised.

"Please, I don't want anything to happen to my almost girlfriend before she becomes my girlfriend," Greg said, smiling and squeezing her hands.

Tabby liked the sound of that, but it was still too early in the relationship for her to say the same.

"Do you need more coffee?" the waitress asked, showing up out of nowhere.

"No, just the bill, thank you," Greg answered.

Greg paid the bill despite heavy protest from Tabby. She insisted it was her turn to pick up the tab, but he wouldn't hear of it. They drove to Tabby's apartment. Fink was staring out the second-floor window across the street when they pulled in to the parking lot.

"I'm going upstairs to check the apartment," Greg insisted, leading the way.

The door was slightly open.

"Oh no, not again," Tabby sighed, tearing up.

"Stay here," Greg ordered.

He disappeared inside, and all was quiet.

9

"You can come in," Greg yelled after he turned on all the lights.

"Where are Ghost and Marmalade?" Tabby questioned in a panic, afraid that they got out through the open apartment door.

They heard a faint meowing in the bathroom and Tabby raced to open the door. Ghost was curled up in the sink. Marmalade sauntered over to Tabby, stretching upwards to show that she wanted to be picked up.

"I'm so glad you guys are okay," Tabby said, gathering up Marmalade close and giving Ghost a pat on the head. "Come get supper, you two."

Greg was looking around.

"Where are the blueprints you took from Mr. Well's house?" he asked.

Tabby put Marmalade down in front of the food dish and ran for the small bedroom.

"They're gone," she yelled from the other room. "He took the blueprints."

"Where is the set you took from his office?"

"They are still in my purse," Tabby confirmed.

Nothing was out of place in the kitchen or living room. It looked just like it had been when they left earlier. Tabby walked to the front window. Across the street, Fink was gone from the upstairs window, and the light had been turned off. She walked to her bedroom but found everything just as she left it.

"Whoever broke in here was obviously looking for the bear," Greg noted. "He's going to figure out that you have it on you since it wasn't found here. The blueprints were a bonus find for him."

"I think so, too. But this is so different from the first break-in. The apartment wasn't trashed like last time. Why did he put the kittens in the bathroom? The door was left open at Mr. Well's house. Calypso could have got out, and the intruder didn't care," Tabby noted, still checking around. "I'm going to call the sheriff and tell him everything. This is getting too dangerous."

She quickly placed the call before she chickened out. He arrived at the apartment in less than ten minutes, and they proceeded to inform him of everything that had transpired within the past forty-eight hours. He was not happy that Tabby had taken the blueprint with her the night Richard had disappeared. She didn't mention that she took the ones from Fink's office when she saw how mad he got about the first set. Tabby reluctantly removed the bear, and the key from her purse as Greg explained how they found them. Since Mr. Wells had given the bear to her, Tabby didn't think to look inside until Greg suggested it. They explained the numbers on the key matched the numbers handwritten on the back of the stolen blueprints.

"Something in that safety deposit box is very important to Larry Fink," Tabby stated, nervously.

"I'm worried that he has figured out that Tabby has the bear on her. I think he will go after her next," Greg admitted, slipping his arm around her waist.

The sheriff smiled when he saw how protective Greg was toward Tabby. He breathed a small sigh of relief that someone would be watching over her.

"Sheriff, doesn't it seem weird to you how neat this break-in was compared to the other one?" Tabby asked. "It's almost like this one was done by a different person."

"I was thinking the same thing," he agreed.

"On Monday morning I am calling my alarm company to alarm this whole building," Greg stated.

The sheriff walked to the back door. He checked the door frame.

"No jimmy marks. Someone had a key to get in here," he concluded. "The only one I can think of is Fink."

"I'll have to take another day off from work and have all the locks changed," Tabby decided.

"We saw Fink at the Outdoor Café tonight with some dark-haired woman. They took off running when he spotted us watching them," Greg admitted. "Our waitress told us Fink eats there almost every night. This was the first time she had seen the woman that was with him."

"We didn't get a good look at her face," Tabby added.

"I'm going to pay Fink a call tomorrow," the sheriff confirmed as he was leaving. "Be sure to lock the doors, even though it won't make much difference since Fink has a key to the place. Be careful."

The sheriff left. Tabby took two wine coolers out of the fridge and offered one to Greg. They sat on the couch with the lights off, watching to see if Fink would appear in the window across the street. The kittens hopped up on the couch. Ghost crawled up on Greg's shoulder and fell asleep as Marmalade made herself comfortable on Tabby's lap.

"That is the first time Ghost has snuggled with anyone," Tabby observed. "I think he likes you."

"I like him, too," Greg said, patting the kitten. "What I don't like is you here by yourself tonight. Fink must have figured out you have the bear with you by now. If you are home, so is the bear. He may come in while you are sleeping."

"When I was little my mom used to alarm our house at night. I think it was because she never got over her hippie fear of the government showing up in the middle of the night and dragging you away to some unknown place never to be seen again. She would take canned goods and made a pyramid with them in front of the door. Then she would balance a pan on the top so if the door was opened the whole thing would fall and make lots of noise to warn us of an intruder."

"I wondered where the name Flower came from, and now I know," Greg commented.

"Yes, she was a hippie back then and still is. If Fink gets by my alarm system, this will be sure to stop him," Tabby assured, getting up off the couch and pulling an old cast iron frying pan out of the kitchen cabinet.

"I guess I don't have to worry about you," Greg acknowledged, laughing.

"I can protect myself, most of the time anyway," Tabby stated. "I am going to have to skip church tomorrow morning. I don't want to leave the place empty for too long and give someone a chance to come back."

"Now that I know you can protect yourself tonight, I will be heading home," Greg said, getting up from the couch.

Tabby stood up and followed him to the door. Greg turned around and leaned against the door frame.

"So, you did consider this a second date tonight?" he asked again, just to be sure.

"Yes, I did," Tabby answered, looking into his eyes.

"Good," he said, gently kissing her on the cheek. "I'll check on you tomorrow."

As Tabby closed the door, her cheek felt like a million electrical charges were pulsing through it. She could hear Greg waiting on the other side, and as soon as he heard the clicks of the two locks, he left for home. Grabbing another wine cooler from the fridge, she stood in the front window watching Greg drive up Main Street.

She wondered if love at first sight was possible. But that was crazy, she hadn't even known him for a whole week yet. Here she was getting ahead of herself again. Once his car was out of sight, she built a pyramid of cans at each door and topped it with an aluminum pan. She didn't think Fink would be stupid enough to break in twice in one night but wasn't going to take any chances.

Ghost and Marmalade followed her around the house. Tabby put the bear and her purse with the blueprints in it in the bedroom next to the bed. The frying pan was placed at an arm's reach from where she would be sleeping. She shut off the lights in the apartment, closed her bedroom door, and propped up a shower curtain rod against the edge of the door so it would fall and alert her if anyone tried to get in.

The kittens jumped up and settled in on the extra pillow next to Tabby's head. Luckily, the night passed uneventfully, and the sun shining into her eyes woke her up early the next morning. She decided not to waste the day away.

Mac's opened at eight. She was in line buying fresh strawberries, blueberries, and raspberries for her first attempt at making her grandmother's jelly when Larry Fink walked briskly into the store.

I need to push him into making a mistake. I just know he has Mr. Wells hidden somewhere. This is probably not the safest thing to do, but here goes.

While he stood watching her from the service desk, Tabby pulled the bear out of her purse pretending it was in the way of her wallet. Fink's eyes went right to the bear. She crammed it back in her purse after she was sure he saw it. He left the store, not waiting for what he came in for.

Now, let's see what he does.

Tabby called Greg on her cell phone on the way home to share what had just happened. He was not happy about the stunt she had just pulled. She assured him she would lock the doors while she made her jelly. Since Jen was coming over to visit and have supper, Tabby would not be alone for most of the day. Greg was more concerned about her being alone at night, and he promised to call her later in the evening to check on her.

She arrived home, locked the doors as promised, and began her preparations for jelly making. Gram's recipes had been hidden in Tabby's bible and luckily, whoever broke into her old apartment had just thrown the bible aside not bothering with anything in it. She pulled the cards out and said a little thank you to her gram for providing her the chance to start her own business. She opened the windows facing Main Street so the wonderful aroma of the jellies would fill the town as they cooked. It would also send the message that Jellies, Jams, and Weddings was underway.

When Jen arrived around three, Tabby had already finished six batches of jellies. The jars were cooling on the table in the second bedroom.

"Everyone could smell the jelly cooking down at the church," Jen informed her. "If you took it out on the street right now, I'm sure you would sell every jar."

"The batch I am making right now is to fill little jars as gifts to the locals for helping me out the way they did," Tabby replied. "I'll pass them out during the week as I run into people."

"What is in the recipes that makes Gram's jellies and jams so good?"

"That's a secret. If everyone knew the secret ingredients, then her jelly wouldn't be so special. Someday, I'll tell you. I'm sure Gram would have trusted you with the recipes. After all, you were like her second granddaughter," Tabby replied, pulling a sterilized hot jar out of its water bath and filling it with jelly mixture.

"Are you going to the meeting at the library tonight?" Jen asked. "I missed last weeks."

"Don't worry. They didn't forget you," Tabby said, laughing. "You and I are co-chairman of the Blue-Ribbon Committee."

"I knew I would get drafted for some committee even though I wasn't there," Jen groaned.

"I was planning on going, but I can't leave the house tonight," Tabby stated.

She explained to her friend what she did at Mac's that morning and caught her up on everything that had happened in the last few days.

"Always in the middle of trouble," Jen lectured, shaking her head.

"I was thinking," Tabby said. "Do you remember that fight I heard between Mr. Pierce and Larry Fink? What if Pierce was saying drive-in and not driving?"

"Do you think he was mixed up in this whole thing somehow?" Jen asked, pouring more wine.

"It's possible. I'm going to do a little investigating on my own and find out who Mr. Pierce really was and what his involvement was in this drive-in thing. Greg volunteered to go to the deeds office and get more information on the sale of the drive-in."

"You've dragged Greg into your love of mysteries, huh? Is he a willing participant?"

"I think he likes it as much as I do," Tabby confirmed.

Jellies, Jams, and Bodies

"You've been spending a lot of time together. I told you I thought he liked you," Jen reminded her.

"I do enjoy the time I spend with him," Tabby admitted.

"I guess you won't be single for too long," Jen said, smiling at her friend.

"We'll see," Tabby evaded. "How do you want your steak done?"

As the friends ate, they chatted about more pleasant things and there was no more discussion of mysteries or kidnappings. They polished off a bottle of wine and opened another one. The local gossip was discussed. Jen informed Tabby that Damian was staying in Scotland and that they ended their relationship.

As Tabby set the dessert down on the table, her cell phone chirped. It was Greg checking on her and making sure she wasn't alone. He told her that he had called his alarm company and they would be out to install an alarm at her place at eleven o'clock on Monday morning. She told him she had run into Tully at Mac's while she was shopping, and he promised to be at her house by nine to change the locks. Everything was working out perfectly. She said goodnight, and he promised to call her the next afternoon from the flower shop. After dessert was finished, Jen gave her friend a hug, and she left to the meeting at the library.

The night passed with no unexpected visits. Tabby was up early the next day to go to the cable office and explain to her boss why she needed the day off. It was short notice, but it was necessary. She walked in, and a young man was sitting in her chair at the first window.

"Hi, Tabs," a cheerful Patti said from the second window. "What are you doing here?"

"I was working here, I thought," Tabby answered, looking at her occupied seat at window one.

"Didn't you get my dad's message?"

"No, what message and when?"

"He left a message on your phone earlier this morning. While you were off this past weekend, we started to train Brian to fill your shoes. Oh yeah, this is Brian Pyle. Brian, this is Tabby. Dad figured with Mr. Pierce's sudden death, you would be able to rent the shop earlier than planned. Brian filled out an application a while ago, so we called him and he started training on Saturday."

"You mean I don't work here anymore?" Tabby asked in a shocked voice.

"Well, technically I guess you do. Dad gave you an early out if you want to take it. He smelled the jelly cooking on his way home from church yesterday and decided to give you a call this morning. You can quit today, with no two-week notice and start setting up your shop. Personally, I think he can't wait to get his hands on some of your gram's jelly," Patti confided with a grin.

"This is awesome!" Tabby declared. "Things couldn't have worked out better for me. I was coming in today to ask for the day off. My new place was broken into, and I had to be home today so Tully could change all the locks. An alarm company is coming to safeguard my shop and apartment right after the locks are changed. I had planned to submit my two weeks' notice this week."

"Dad beat you to it, but he wants one of the first jars of jelly in exchange," Patti said, giving Tabby a hug. "I'll miss working with you. Get that shop up and running before tourist season is in full swing."

"I will. Tell your dad he's first on my list for jelly delivery," Tabby confirmed. "Nice meeting you, Brian. I have to run."

I can't believe it! I'm my own boss now. No more cable company...woohoo!

Back home, Tabby waited for Tully to arrive. She poured herself a second cup of coffee and began working online to order wedding supplies for her store. Her computer desk had been set up in the front corner of the living room, next to the window. She could see up and down Main Street while seated there. When Tully's truck pulled up, Larry Fink was watching out the front door of his realtor's office. Tabby could tell by the look on Fink's face that he was none too happy with the locksmith being there. She watched as he picked up his cell phone and called someone.

Tully changed the locks on the apartment's back door, the shop's front and back doors, and the connecting doors from the shop to the upstairs apartment. He finished just as the alarm company showed up.

"I'll make you a deal. Give me a couple of jars of Gram's Blueberry

Sin Jelly, and I'll send you a bill for services after you've opened the shop and have some money coming in," Tully stated.

"Seriously? It's a deal," Tabby agreed, heading to the second bedroom to grab two jars of jelly. "Thanks, Tully. This makes me feel so much safer."

You would have thought she gave Tully a million dollars the way he hugged those two jars of jelly. Tabby was beginning to gain confidence that her business was going to be a success. Tully left, and Tabby turned her attention to the alarm company.

The installer walked her through what he thought would be the best way to alarm the whole building. All windows and doors on the first floor would have sensors on them. The backstairs door to the apartment would also be alarmed. As Tabby was looking over the monthly charges the installer wrote up for her to approve, she felt a tap on her shoulder. She turned and was face to face with Larry Fink.

10

"What do you think you are doing?" Fink demanded.

"Excuse me?" Tabby asked innocently.

"You haven't even signed a rental lease yet, and you are changing everything like the building is yours," an irate Fink insisted.

Now you care about the rental because you won't be able to get into the building to get the bear.

"It is mine. Mr. Wells said so," Tabby confirmed.

"And how did he do that? He's not even here," the realtor replied in a menacing tone.

"Yes, let's talk about that, shall we? Mr. Wells disappears mysteriously, and all of a sudden you are giving people fake tax hike bills and in charge of all the rentals again. The whole town knows that you were fired as his agent. How convenient for you that he is nowhere to be found and you are in charge of everything again," Tabby stated, standing up to him and showing no sign of fear.

"Are you accusing me of something?" he hissed, getting right in Tabby's face.

"If the shoe fits…" Tabby answered, pushing back.

"You smug little…"

"Back off, Fink," Greg yelled from the stairs.

Greg finished running up the stairs, two at a time, and pushed his way in between Tabby and the imminent threat. The realtor took several steps backward.

"What do you think you're doing?" Greg demanded.

"Nothing that can't be taken care of in the near future," Fink answered smugly, glaring at Tabby as he headed for the door.

"I'm not paying that rent hike you delivered this morning," Greg called out as Fink slinked down the stairs. "Not until I talk to Mr. Wells about it."

"Larry Fink has Mr. Wells hidden somewhere, I'm sure of it now. He's trying to make all the money he can with those fake tax bills and rent hikes, and then I think he is going to disappear for good," Tabby surmised. "I just wish I could figure out the drive-in angle."

"I think you're right. I stopped at the deed office this morning. It seems Marsha Swanson died one month after her husband did and her brother was supposed to inherit the drive-in. Guess who was named the beneficiary in the will instead?"

"It had to be Larry Fink," Tabby stated. "Why would Marsha change her mind and leave the property to Fink?"

"Good question," Greg said.

"What are you doing here? Isn't your shop open?" Tabby asked.

"I was on my lunch hour and decided to come see how things were going."

"I'm glad you did. Fink was getting a little too close for my liking," Tabby stated.

Greg put his arm around her waist and pulled her close. This time, she responded by putting her arms around his neck.

"I don't want anything to happen to my girl," he whispered in her ear.

"Miss Moon...uh, oh, sorry for the interruption," the alarm agent said, looking down at his clipboard. "Mr. Stone, I'll come back later."

"It's okay. What do you need?"

"I need her signature on the work order so we can start installing the system. It is in the paperwork she was looking over. It should take about two hours to complete."

Jellies, Jams, and Bodies

"Are you going to feel safe with the system they are putting in?" Greg inquired, turning to Tabby.

"Yes, it's a good system. Where do you need me to sign?"

He took the clipboard and indicated the places that required her signature.

"We'll get to work. I'll collect the deposit when the system is up and running, and I have shown you how to use it," he confirmed, taking the clipboard back.

Greg hung around for a little while longer. Tabby told him about the cable company cutting her loose so that she would be free to work on her shop.

While they were working on the alarm system, Tabby was going to begin to box up some of the baseball inventory that Mr. Pierce left behind. She had stopped at Mac's Market on the way home from the cable company and picked up some empty boxes. Greg told her to pile the filled boxes at the top of the stairs, and he would carry them down into the cellar after his shop closed. He invited her to dinner, and as she agreed, he gave her a quick kiss on the cheek and headed back to his shop.

Since Tabby didn't want Ghost and Marmalade to get out while the windows and doors were open, she hustled them into the bathroom. This was the only room not included in the installation of the alarm system. She walked down the connecting stairs to begin transforming the baseball shop into the Jellies, Jams, and Weddings shop.

Tabby stood in the middle of the space, and the reality hit her that it was hers. Tears filled her eyes as her dreams were finally coming true. All that time scrimping and saving had at last paid off. Tabby was standing in what was now her own shop on Main Street. She was truly sorry Mr. Pierce had to die for her to be open for the busy summer season, but if she worked hard and kept at it, she just might have her grand opening in June.

Mr. Pierce had filled the shelves to bursting, and it was going to take several days to box things up and move everything downstairs. With him gone, Tabby would use the already installed shelving units and the new counter. When she found out who everything would go to in his family, she would offer to pay for the fixtures to keep them in her shop.

Suddenly, Tabby remembered the telescope and the listening devices. She ran for the back room where she had last seen them. The telescope was still there, but the black recording box and headphones were missing.

Fink must have taken them. Who else would know what they were being used for?

Tabby returned to boxing up the baseball items. She was deep in thought as to what could have been on the recording devices when a knock on the front door made her jump. Sheriff Puckett was peering in through the glass, so Tabby waved him inside.

"You have a big job ahead of you," he said, looking around. "What are you going to do with all this baseball stuff?"

"Larry Fink, of all people, suggested I put it in the cellar," Tabby answered. "The problem is, I don't know what to do with the stuff afterward. I have looked online and can't find any information on Mr. Pierce or his family. The lease signed by him is still in Fink's possession, so I can't see who he listed as his emergency contacts."

"I came to tell you that I pulled Fink in for questioning. He claims that Richard had a change of mind when he found out that pulling his business out of Fink's office would bankrupt him."

"I seriously doubt that," Tabby mumbled. "I'm not signing any lease or paying Fink a cent until Mr. Wells is found and I clear everything with him."

"I doubt it, too. But, without Richard being here, I can't do anything. My hands are tied."

"Did you ask him about the fake tax bills he's been handing out to everyone who rents in town?" Tabby inquired.

"He claims that they are legitimate increases as Richard hadn't adjusted anyone's rents in years. Again, I can't prove or disprove what he says. I have filed a subpoena to get Richard's files and leases on the grounds of fraud and embezzlement. I'm waiting to hear back from the judge in Larsen."

Tabby told the sheriff what Greg had discovered at the deed office.

Fink had inherited the drive-in property and quickly divided it and sold the bigger piece off to a developing company.

"How the heck did Fink end up in the Swanson's will?"

"That's what we were trying to figure out. Maybe that's what Mr. Wells knew, and that's why they had to make him disappear," Tabby suggested. "Speaking of disappearing, I also noticed that the recording device that Mr. Pierce had in the backroom is gone, too."

"I'm going to check into some things, and I'll get back to you. I am relieved that you are installing alarms in the entire building. It makes me feel better. I worry about you," the fatherly sheriff replied. "Greg can't be here all the time looking after you. Just want to say you two make a nice-looking couple."

Tabby blushed and didn't say a word.

"I'll be in touch," he confirmed, leaving Tabby to her work.

Finally, the alarm system was installed, and Tabby was instructed how to use it. There were two separate systems—one for upstairs and one for downstairs, just like at Jen's place. She set the alarm and then disarmed each level several times to make sure she was comfortable with what she was doing. As agreed, Tabby paid the deposit for all the equipment and the first month up front.

She locked the front and back door to the shop and let the kittens out of the bathroom. They followed her down the stairs to the shop and explored while she worked. The afternoon passed quickly as Tabby filled nineteen boxes with baseball merchandise. She decided to take the lighter boxes down to the cellar by herself. Before she knew it, she had moved all nineteen boxes downstairs and stacked them on pallets in the far corner.

The patches on the wall caught her attention again. She walked around, banging on each spot. They sounded solid and didn't give way when she thumped on them. While checking out the walls, Tabby noticed the wood paneling under the stairs looked slightly different from the rest of the paneling in the cellar. She tapped on the discolored partition. This time, she heard a hollow echo coming from behind where she tapped.

This paneling has been replaced. Let's see why.

She went upstairs to get her hammer and flashlight. Tabby pried the top left corner of the paneling away from the wall. She turned on her flashlight and peered into the dark space. Tabby gasped and inhaled the revolting stench coming from the hole. She dropped the flashlight and left the hammer wedged between the wall and the paneling. Tabby couldn't get up the stairs fast enough to pull out her cell phone and dial the sheriff's number.

Sheriff Puckett arrived in under two minutes, along with Deputy Small. The coroner's wagon pulled up minutes later.

"Tabby are you okay?" he asked.

"I'm fine, just a bit shocked. I wasn't expecting to find another dead body in my shop," Tabby replied, still clutching her cell phone.

"Where is it?" the deputy questioned.

"It's down in the cellar under the stairs, behind the paneling. I think the hammer is still wedged in the wall," Tabby replied, sitting down on a box. "I'll stay up here if you don't mind. The smell is awful."

The two men descended the stairs and then she heard the sounds of the paneling being ripped away from the wall. The coroner came in, and she directed him toward the cellar. A crowd was gathering outside. Tabby's mom and Greg came flying through the front door of the shop at the same time.

"Oh, Tabby, thank God you are all right," her mom exclaimed, seeing her daughter seated on the box.

Greg reacted more emotionally. He grabbed her hands, picked her up, and hugged her until she couldn't breathe.

"I saw the coroner's wagon. All I could think of was Fink had gotten to you," Greg stated, his face riddled with fear.

"I'm fine. But I will need the wagon if you don't loosen your grip on me so I can breathe," Tabby interrupted as she tried to inject some humor into the moment.

"What in heaven's name is going on?" her mom demanded to know.

"I found another dead body down in the cellar," her daughter answered.

"I don't know if I want you to stay in this shop or even this building," Samantha said, shaking her head. "It's bad Karma."

"Another body?" Greg repeated.

"Yes, a woman's body. I didn't recognize her. But, then again, I didn't stick around long enough to get a really good look."

Sheriff Puckett slowly climbed the stairs and walked to where Tabby was sitting.

"I don't know who she is. The coroner says she's been in there about three months. He's going to remove the body and then run her dental records and fingerprints."

"Well, that rules out Mr. Pierce as a suspect. He had only been in the building a little over a month. Everything points right back to Fink again. He's the only one, besides Mr. Wells, who had a key to this place the six months it was empty" Tabby reasoned.

The coroner and his assistant walked by with the gurney and a body bag. They transported the bag down to the cellar and left the gurney at the top of the stairs. Several minutes later they returned, placing the now full body bag on the gurney, and wheeling it out of the shop. The horrific smell from the cellar was slowly making its way upstairs. Tabby held her nose at the repugnant stench.

"The smell will dissipate now that the body has been removed. There is nothing else in the hole behind the wall to help us figure out who she was. I think she was killed somewhere else and dumped there. No purse, no jewelry, no nothing," the sheriff stated. "The place was empty except for the body."

"Can I close the hole back up again?" Tabby requested.

"The deputies can close it up for you if you'd like. The smell in the hole will eventually be absorbed into the dirt. Once it is sealed up, the stink in the cellar should be gone in a week or so. It might benefit you to open the small windows in the foundation to help air it out."

The two deputies returned to the cellar. Tabby and Greg sat upstairs listening to the hammering. The young couple looked over, and Gladys Twittle had her face pressed against the front window. Her facial features were so distorted from being pressed flat against the glass that they both burst out laughing. She had no idea that they were laughing at her and continued her quest for the next batch of gossip she would share tomorrow morning at The Cup.

The hole was sealed, and the sheriff and his deputies left. Tabby's mom absolutely refused to go near the cellar door. She didn't want her aura penetrated by any evil residue that was left down there, her hippie way of thinking coming through again. Samantha kissed her daughter and left to reopen her own shop.

They shut off the light and closed the cellar door.

"I wouldn't put any stock down there until the odor is completely gone," Greg advised. "It might pick up the smell."

"I'm going to keep boxing the baseball stuff up, but I'll put the boxes in the back room until the smell is gone. I'm not putting any of my new stock down there either. I'll keep it upstairs in the second bedroom for now," Tabby stated.

Greg walked over to Tabby. He stared at her without saying anything.

"What? What did I do?" Tabby asked, confused.

"You have no idea how scared I was when I saw the coroner's wagon come rushing by my shop and stop here. I don't even remember telling Sally I was leaving. I ran out the front door and didn't stop running until I came through that door and saw you sitting there, safe."

"I should have called you and told you I was okay. I'm sorry I didn't. I wasn't thinking too straight when I looked in the hole, and a face was looking back at me."

Greg reached out and took both her hands in his.

"I know it hasn't even been a month since we have known each other, but I love you, Tabitha Flower Moon. I'm just like my dad. We Stones fall hard and fast. I can wait for you to see we belong together, no matter how long it takes. You don't have to say anything now. I just wanted you to know how I feel."

She reached up and stroked his face. His eyes told her he was telling the truth.

They kissed. The world around them had faded away until it was just the two of them together and Gladys Twittle watching them through the window.

11

The next couple of weeks passed by quickly. Every morning when Tabby woke up, her first thoughts were of Mr. Wells. Before she climbed out of bed, she would say a little prayer for his safe return.

The mornings were spent making batches of jelly and the afternoons, setting up her shop. She had passed out all her small thank-you jars, and the locals were counting the days until her shop opened. Orders from the Main Street businesses were pouring in, and she wasn't even open yet. She was going to have to hire someone to work the shop full time so she could make jelly every morning to keep up with the demand. She put a "Help Wanted" sign in the front window.

Tabby put paper up in the front windows so no one could look in as she was setting up the interior of the shop. She wanted the grand opening to be a surprise for everyone.

Every night, Greg and Tabby ate supper together, sometimes at the diner and sometimes at her apartment. He never let her pay when they went out to eat. Being with Greg was so different than her time with Finn. Greg treated her like royalty. She wondered when the other shoe would drop, and the special treatment would end.

Tabby had free time during the day because of her store not being open yet. She would bring Greg lunch, and they would eat next to the frog fountain. He loved the fountain more than she ever could have. She finally learned the frogs' names. The top level was Bernard and Frederick. The frogs on the second level were William and Stanley. The level right above the lily pond had Roberto and Ulrich playing in the water. The lone frog sitting on a lily pad in the pond was Horatio.

It was amazing how many people would come to the flower shop to eat lunch next to the frog fountain. Some days, there was nowhere for Tabby and Greg to sit. They would walk across the street and sit under the gazebo on the town green to eat. They had become a well-known couple around town.

They were inseparable. Even Jen told Tabby she had never seen her happier than when she was with Greg. Samantha Moon adored Greg, and she couldn't have been more thrilled that her daughter and the flower shop owner were a couple.

It was Sunday night and the last meeting before Summer Kick-Off Weekend. The committee agreed to have the last meeting at the diner. They had added another fourteen volunteers since the first meeting and had outgrown the room at the library. Greg had been bamboozled by Tabby's mom into joining the committee. He pretended to be angry but was secretly enjoying the time spent with the locals getting to know everyone.

Jen sat on one side of Tabby and Greg on the other. Sitting on the other side of Jen was her new boyfriend, Alex Keyes. They had been spending a lot of time together at the bookstore. Tabby really liked him and was happy that Jen had found someone after her long-distance break-up with Damian.

"Welcome to the last meeting before Summer Kick-Off next weekend," Tom Montgomery, the owner of the diner announced. "Has anyone had any problems completing what they needed to get done?"

A chorus of "nos" filled the air.

"Good. We will all meet on the green at seven o'clock on Saturday morning. Stan and some of the other guys are setting up the booths and fences on Friday night. Tabby and Jen, you have three areas to set up. Let us know if you need any extra help. The weatherman says it is going to be a beautiful weekend. No rain in sight," Tom happily proclaimed.

"Mr. Montgomery, do you have the children's compositions so Jen and I can start reading them over the coming week?" Tabby inquired.

"They are right here," Tom replied, reaching into his briefcase and handing a pile of papers to Tabby.

"Wow! There's a lot of entries this year," Jen exclaimed. "Good thing we have a whole week to read them and some extra help," she said, squeezing Alex's hand.

"Here are the ribbons that need to be hung near the winning compositions. Blue for first, white for second, and red for third. Three different age groups are listed on a piece of paper in the ribbon bag. This second bag of ribbons is for the other contests—quilts, pies, and canning."

The meals were served, and Samantha said grace over the table. She asked that Mr. Wells be kept safe wherever he was and that he be returned to the people that loved him. As everyone said amen, talk at the table turned to Mr. Wells and the fact that he had been missing for almost a month now, the sheriff still having no leads in his disappearance.

Conversations turned to laughter and teasing as everyone enjoyed their homemade dinners. Two hours later the meeting ended, and it was another successful year on the books. Wes Garcia and Tommy Wilbur, owners of the Tilted Coffee Cup, volunteered to be co-presidents for next year.

Jen and Alex were going to Baily's Bar and Grill for a couple of drinks and invited Tabby and Greg to join them. Greg said he had to decline their invitation as he had an early truck delivery arriving at five in the morning. Unlike the other three who lived in town, he had to drive to Larsen and then back first thing in the morning.

He walked Tabby home and made sure she was safely tucked inside her apartment. He kissed her until she felt her heart would bust out of her chest and then mentioned that he would see her for lunch the next day. She set the upstairs alarm and sat down to drink a wine cooler. Sitting in the dark, she could see Fink moving around in his upstairs apartment. He was on his cell phone talking to someone. The lights went out, and Tabby couldn't see him anymore.

Since the kittens had slept most of the day away, they were tearing through the apartment with excess feline energy to burn. Ghost jumped onto the plant tower in the front window. The plant on the bottom shelf tipped on its side. He jumped onto the second and third shelves where there were no plants. He reached the top shelf and sent the plant flying into the front window.

"Bad kittens," Tabby scolded, getting up to rescue her plants.

Ghost was sitting on the top shelf looking innocently down at her. She tapped him on the butt and put him down on the floor. He jumped right back up to the top again. Before she could react, he curled up in a ball on the top shelf and closed his eyes.

"I guess this is going to be a cat tower instead of a plant tower from now on," Tabby grumbled as she moved the plants on the other shelves to the kitchen table.

She cleaned up the spilled dirt. Ghost slept through the whole thing, happily perched on the top of the plant stand. Marmalade followed Tabby wherever she went, meowing loudly at her until she leaned down and picked up the orange kitten. Marmalade's purring sounded like a motorboat through a megaphone.

"You are such a love bug," Tabby crooned, hugging the tiny kitten. "You and your brother are nothing alike, but I love you both dearly."

Tabby grabbed another wine cooler, turned the lights off again, and sat in the recliner looking out the front window. Marmalade sprung up into her lap and began meticulously cleaning herself. It was ten thirty, but Tabby wasn't tired. She couldn't get her mind off Mr. Wells. She was worried sick about him. At his age, she didn't know how long he would last in captivity. She hoped his tenacity would see him through until he was found.

"I think I need some fresh air," Tabby decided, setting the cat down on the floor.

She grabbed a blanket, set the alarm, and set out for the town green. When she was younger, she and her mom would lay on the green at night and watch the stars. Tabby had tried to get Finn to lay there with her, but after five minutes he was done with the idea and called it stupid. She hadn't been back to the green to look at the stars since that miserable night with Finn two summers ago. It was time to return and look at the stars once again.

It was only a three-minute walk from her place and right in the center of town. She hadn't seen Fink since their last run in when she was changing the locks on her building. What were the chances she would run into him this time of night?

Tabby spread out the blanket next to the gazebo. She was on the far side, in the dark, away from the street lights of Main Street. She lay there, in the quiet of the night, trying to find the stars her mom used to point out to her when she was little. Just as she was beginning to relax, she heard footsteps on the wooden floor of the gazebo. Someone was talking on a cell phone, and that someone was Larry Fink. Not wanting to be discovered, she lay perfectly still, hardly daring to breathe.

I know what I said, but I changed my mind.

Tabby could hear someone yelling on the other end of the phone, but she couldn't make out what the person was saying.

I'm done with this town. It's getting too risky to stay here. The sheriff has questioned me twice. The locals won't pay the fake tax bills I have been handing out. It's time to move on. This Friday, the demolition will wipe out all traces of evidence. The Swansons are dead, and so is Pierce. Wells is still alive, but soon he will be dead like the others. There will be no one left to know what we did or how we did it. No, I don't want to know exactly where he is so I can go watch. Sometimes you scare me.

The voice on the other end of the phone was still screaming and obviously furious with Fink.

We scammed over a million dollars from this town. That should hold us over until we can come up with something new somewhere else. The sale of the drive-in property netted us almost a million dollars in cash alone.

Tabby strained to listen to the other voice on the phone and thought it sounded like a woman's voice. It could be the dark-haired woman Fink was going to eat supper with that night at the café.

Friday morning, you can give Wells his last dose of drugs. He will sleep right through everything going on around him and never wake up again. I will be in the office all morning getting things together to leave. I'll be gone by noon. I know, I know, don't forget the pictures. Yeah, are you sure the money is safe? Seriously? The old man is sleeping right on top of it and doesn't have a clue it's even there?

A cricket jumped on Tabby and scared the heck out of her. She fought back a scream and hoped Fink didn't hear her moving. He continued on with his conversation and she realized she was safe.

I think I want to retire with my fifty percent. One of these times I'm not going to be so lucky. I'm the front man. You are always in the background, sitting behind your safe little desk, and no one even realizes you are in on the scam. What do you mean I'm an idiot? No. I'm the smart one. I know when to get out and stay out. After this weekend, you are on your own. I have to go. Someone is coming up the sidewalk. Talk to you tomorrow.

Fink walked away from the gazebo toward home. Tabby let out a huge breath when she knew he was out of hearing distance. She sat up and peeked over the edge of the gazebo to make sure Fink was out of sight. Sure that he was gone, she stood up, shook out her blanket, and ran for home. She ran up the back stairs and to the front window of her apartment.

The lights in Fink's apartment were on. He was home again. Fink wasn't going anywhere tonight. He himself stated that he didn't know where Mr. Wells was and even if he did, he wouldn't say because the money was hidden with him and would be confiscated. Friday was his day to escape. He had no idea his conversation had been overheard at the gazebo, so he had no reason to run.

She sat in the recliner trying to calm herself down after her encounter. Tabby closed her eyes and slowed her breathing. She didn't mean to, but she dozed off and didn't wake up until four-thirty.

She jumped up out of the chair and reached for her phone. She talked to dispatch who said that she should meet the sheriff at the station in the next twenty minutes. There was no sign of anyone awake in Fink's apartment as Tabby hurried up the street.

The sheriff, looking half awake, was just pouring himself his first cup of coffee as Tabby started to relate every word she had heard at the gazebo. Sheriff Puckett was glad to hear Richard Wells was still alive but was mad at Tabby for wandering around by herself in the middle of the night.

With all this new information, it was time to bring Larry Fink in and find out just what was going on. Deputy Small had just checked in for work, and the two men left for Larry Fink's apartment. Tabby followed behind but veered off to her apartment so she could watch from her front window.

She called Greg to catch him up on what was going on. He was understandably angry when he found out that Tabby had ventured outside alone late at night. The sheriff came out of Fink's place and was waving to Tabby to join him.

"I have to run. Sheriff Puckett is flagging me down from across the street. I'll call you later," Tabby promised, heading for the door.

She reached the sidewalk, and the sheriff put his hand up to stop her.

"You don't want to go in there. Fink is dead. It looks like he got ambushed by someone he knew and let in willingly. He was beat the same way Pierce was—baseball bat to the head."

"It had to be the person on the other end of the phone. Maybe Fink didn't kill anyone. Maybe the other person did all the killing, and we were blaming him," Tabby stated. "Fink wanted out, and she didn't like it, so she took care of him, too. Now she has all the money to herself, and only she knows where the money and Mr. Wells are being hidden."

"This leads us back to where we were before—no closer to finding Richard," the sheriff mumbled. "You should have called me right away, and maybe he'd still be alive."

"I know I should have. I didn't mean to fall asleep. But we have until Friday for whatever is supposed to happen to happen. Don't give up hope. I am certain he hasn't given up on us," Tabby pleaded, trying to sound upbeat.

Sheriff Puckett headed back to the murder scene and Tabby left, deciding she needed a walk to clear her head.

She found herself automatically heading to the flower shop to sit next to her frog fountain. Even though it was in Greg's shop, she still secretly considered it her fountain. Tabby stopped at the Tilted Coffee Cup, picking up two coffees and two blueberry muffins. She had to answer questions about her and Greg's relationship to some of the locals who had been listening to Gladys Twittle's gossip. Tabby set the record straight. She and Greg were dating, but there had been no secret marriage. A smile crossed her lips as she left the coffee shop. Her and Greg's prank had worked so well that Gladys blabbed everything she had overheard that night at the restaurant.

Tabby walked two doors up to the still closed flower shop. As she was walking, the coroner's wagon made its way up Main Street one more time. Nothing had happened in this quiet town for over forty years. Now in less than a month, three murders, with the possibility of four, had caused people to start locking doors that had never been locked before.

Greg had seen the coroner's wagon drive by. He ran out the front door of his shop and almost crashed into Tabby who was arriving with the coffees.

"What happened?" Greg demanded to know.

"Fink's dead. Someone bashed his head in with a baseball bat, just like Pierce's," Tabby answered, handing Greg his coffee. "He let the person in the door and was hit from behind. Fink had to know and trust whoever it was."

"Do you think it was the person he was talking to on the phone?"

"It had to be. Personally, I think it was that dark-haired woman he ran away with that night at the café."

"It's too bad we never got to see her face," Greg sighed.

"I know. I'm going to sit by the fountain and have my coffee and muffin. It relaxes me and helps me to think. I brought a muffin for you, too."

"Thanks, I'll eat it on my break. I have two weddings going out this morning. Sorry, but I don't have time to sit with you right now."

"That's fine. I just need some quiet time near the fountain," Tabby declared.

Tabby chose the bench closest to the fountain. She set her coffee on the floor and stared at the frogs playing in the water. The sound of the water splashing over the steps of the fountain and into the lily pond below calmed her. She had to clear her head. There had to be something she was missing, something that wasn't registering clearly in her thoughts.

Tabby watched as the flowers for the first wedding were hustled out the front door and thought to herself that her arrangements were so much better. No offense to Margaret, but her flowers were lacking that romantic feeling that should be experienced on that very special day. Deep in her heart, she knew that when her own shop opened, Greg would lose some of his business to her arrangements. She felt bad about it, but business was business.

She ran over the current events in her mind, but no new resolutions came to her. Tabby decided to go home and spend the rest of the day cooking batches of jelly. The windows would be left open to tease the town with the wonderful aromas of the filled jars that would be waiting for them when she opened her shop.

Tabby only had a short time to get ready for her grand opening. The next day would be spent cleaning the shop from top to bottom. Mr. Pierce had painted the walls and installed all new fixtures. She decided to go ahead and order a few more stand-alone fixtures that she needed. A new table with four chairs had been delivered for comfortable seating during pre-wedding appointments. Her wedding stock had been delivered and was waiting to be set up on the shelves around the meeting table for easy viewing.

Over the last week, in between everything that had been going on, she managed to make over three hundred jars of jelly. Each batch yielded ten to a dozen jars of the precious gold. Now Tabby would offer the product to the world, or at least to anyone who visited her shop.

"Are you okay?" Greg asked. "You look like you're in La-La land."

"Just thinking about all the work that I have to get done before the shop opens," Tabby answered. "And poor Mr. Wells."

"We'll find him, don't worry," Greg reassured her, squeezing her shoulder. "And I'll help you at night with whatever you need to finish for your shop opening."

"I sure hope so. Have you ever had this sick feeling that you know something, but you just can't put our finger on it?"

"Sometimes. I have the second wedding party coming in shortly. Do you want to have supper at the diner tonight? Say, six-thirty?"

"Yes, sounds good. Tomorrow night supper is at my apartment. Jen and Alex are coming over, too. We need to start reading the compositions the kids submitted for the Summer Kick-Off Weekend. You in?"

"I'm in. I can't get there until six-thirty."

"Supper will be at seven. I'm going home to make jelly. I'll meet you at the diner later."

Greg bent over and kissed her. The tingle was still there just like the first time he kissed her. This time it happened in a public place where she realized that people were watching. While Tabby had sat deep in thought, the flower shop had opened, and customers were milling around.

Mrs. Ryan happened to be walking by the flower shop window when Greg kissed her. As she ran off, Tabby knew that she was making a beeline straight for Gladys Twittle to report what she had just seen. It never ceased to amaze Tabby how both the women could be in the right place at the right time. What were the odds she would be walking by at the exact moment Greg kissed her?

Tabby strolled past the Penny Poor Antique Shop on her way home. Sure enough, Mrs. Ryan was standing at the counter telling Gladys all the juicy details of the public display of affection. Tabby waved at them as she passed the front window. Both women turned their backs to her and continued gossiping.

I imagine that Gladys is probably still pretty steamed about the prank we played on her.

Ghost and Marmalade met Tabby at the door. They followed her around the apartment until she acknowledged them and picked each one up and gave them some loving. She was giving Ghost a rub behind the ears as he had become much friendlier since he had decided that Tabby could be trusted.

"You know, Ghost. I haven't been back to the drive-in to look around since the day we found you two," Tabby whispered to the cat. "I think I will go back there tomorrow morning and poke around."

The kitten tilted his head. It was like he was trying to understand what she was saying to him. Giving up, he laid down in her arms and closed his eyes.

"Oh, no you don't. I have jelly to make," she said, setting the cat on the top step of the plant stand in the front window.

Looking out the front window Tabby could see the yellow police tape that had been placed across the front door of the real estate office. For just a short moment, she felt bad for Larry Fink. Yes, he was a criminal that had bilked many of the locals out of their hard-earned money, but he had been killed by someone he knew and trusted. It had to be the dark-haired woman they saw at the café. How ironic that Fink had protected her identity that night, and she killed him shortly after that.

The next five hours were spent cooking jelly. The open windows allowed the wonderful smells to waft down Main Street. Several people yelled up to her asking when the store was going to open. She was happy with the way things were progressing and the obvious excitement that was building for her grand opening. One hundred jars of jelly were cooling in the spare bedroom. She called it quits for the night and cleaned up the kitchen.

Tabby and Greg had a pleasant supper at the diner. No eavesdropper was sitting in the next booth to listen in on their conversation. When the Twittles did arrive for dinner, Gladys asked to be seated as far away as possible from the young couple. Greg was laughing as Bea sat them at the opposite side of the diner.

They discussed the grand opening of Tabby's shop and made plans for the upcoming Summer Kick-Off Weekend. Greg told Tabby he had found the perfect small house to rent on Emblem Avenue just off West Main Street. The current tenants were moving out by the end of May and Greg hoped that the house would be his for the renting. As far as he knew, he was the only one who had inquired about it so far. Mr. Wells owned the house so everything would be up in the air until he could be found.

Tabby got quiet when Greg mentioned Mr. Wells.

"Don't worry, we'll find him," Greg comforted, as he noticed the sudden change in Tabby's demeanor.

"I am so frustrated! Something in the back of my mind is saying I have the answers, but no matter how hard I try, I can't figure it out," she said, tearing up. "I know Mr. Wells depends on us to find him. I have been so busy that the time has just passed by since he first disappeared. I should have been doing more to find him."

"The sheriff has been working to find him, too, and come up with nothing. Tomorrow night, the four of us will go over the conversation you heard, word for word, and see if together we can come up with an answer."

Greg walked Tabby to her apartment then wrapped his arms around her.

"Don't ever go wandering around in the middle of the night without me by your side," he said. "Tabitha Moon, I don't want anything to happen to you. You are my future."

Tabby remained silent.

"I know you need time, so did my mom. I can wait," Greg promised, kissing her softly. "I'll see you tomorrow night."

Tabby watched him walk away into the dark. Maybe after her shop was up and running and Mr. Wells had been found she could concentrate on her and Greg's relationship. Right now, her life was too hectic.

The kittens met her at the door, rolling around and meowing as they had fallen in the habit of doing. They followed her to the bedroom and waited patiently on the bed as she changed. Ghost settled on the spare pillow and Marmalade crawled onto Tabby's chest. The family fell into a contented sleep.

At two a.m., an alarm sounded.

12

Tabby jumped out of bed as the shop alarm was going off. She grabbed the baseball bat she kept next to the bed and headed for the door connecting the apartment to the downstairs shop. Opening the door ever so slightly, she reached in and turned on the overhead lights. The back door closed with a bang as the phone started ringing in the back room.

She turned off the alarm and answered the phone. It was the alarm company responding to the signal that her alarm had been activated. They wanted to know if she needed the police. Assuring them she was all right and that the intruder was gone, she hung up the phone. The sheriff's car pulled up to the front of the store ten minutes later. Tabby let him in.

"The alarm company called me. What's going on?"

"I told them I didn't need the police, that I was fine. I didn't want to get you out of bed this time of the morning," Tabby said, shaking her head. "Someone broke in. They smashed the window in my workroom, but I think the alarm scared them off. Whoever it was is long gone."

"Is anything missing or disturbed?" he asked.

"There is only one thing missing," she stated firmly.

"One thing?"

"After I gave you the key out of jelly bear, I figured it was safe to put him on top of the register. Mr. Wells wanted him to be the mascot for my shop. Guess what one thing is missing?"

The sheriff looked at the register- the bear was gone.

"Someone is going to be mighty upset when they don't find the key in the bear," the sheriff said, chuckling. "I'd like to be a fly on that wall."

"Me, too," Tabby agreed.

"How did they know the bear was there?" the sheriff asked.

"The front door has been propped open for deliveries this past week. Anyone could have walked by and seen it on the register," Tabby confirmed.

"I'm glad you had the alarm in place. Mr. Stone is going to be a good influence in your life. He still is in your life, right?"

"You're getting as bad as Gladys Twittle," Tabby chided.

"On that ultimate insult, I'll be leaving," the sheriff mumbled. "Be extra careful from here on out. Whoever it was, knows you have found the key and they will come after you next."

"Sheriff Puckett, have you found out who the woman was in the cellar wall yet?" Tabby asked as she walked him to the door.

"Not yet. We are working on matching dental records. Her fingerprints weren't in any database. I promise I will let you know when we have some answers."

The front and back doors of the shop were locked. The alarm couldn't be set because of the broken window. She took a large empty box, flattened it, and crammed it into the window frame. Tabby figured whoever broke in would not return as they got what they had come for: the bear. In the morning, she would call someone to replace the window. The alarm company would have to install another sensor on the new glass.

She couldn't think about crawling into bed again. Tabby didn't want to be sleeping upstairs without an alarm in the shop and a broken window. She made a pot of coffee and started to empty boxes. The kittens were running up and down the stairs, jumping in the emptied boxes, and spreading the packing materials all over the shop. She was able to have the entire wedding area of her shop set up and arranged by seven o'clock. Exhausted, she sat down on the floor and closed her eyes. Marmalade crawled up on Tabby's lap, laid down, and stared at her. Ghost was still jumping in and out of boxes.

Tabby fell asleep. The next thing she remembered was someone knocking on the front door of the shop. Jolted out of her sleep, she stared at the front door while trying to remember where she was and why she was sleeping on the floor. Marmalade jumped off her lap. She unlocked the door and found Greg standing there.

"Are you okay? Sheriff Puckett came by the shop and told me what happened," he asked, giving her a quick kiss on the cheek.

"I'm okay. What time is it?"

"It's noon. I was on my lunch hour and decided I had better check on you."

"I fell asleep on the floor. Crap. I wanted to call early this morning to get the window fixed. I needed to call the alarm company, too. Half the day has been wasted," Tabby sighed.

"I think the sheriff went by the hardware store early this morning to tell them you needed a new window. The alarm company is only twenty minutes away. I am sure they can get the alarm back up for tonight."

"I hope so. I guess I'm grumpy from falling asleep on the hard floor and frustrated because today is Wednesday and I am running out of time to find Mr. Wells."

"The other reason I am here is to tell you that Jen has to pass on tonight. She wants to know if we can get together tomorrow night instead. She has a meeting after the store closes with some big-time author about setting up a book signing."

"That only leaves us one night to read all the entries. I guess with four of us we can get through them. I'll go talk to Jen later. I haven't talked with her much lately since I have been so busy with the shop."

"I won't come visit you tonight after work. You need to get some rest. I'll call you in the morning," Greg said.

"I so agree. My bed and I are going to be best friends tonight providing the alarm is fixed. I'll be at your shop in the morning with coffee and muffins," Tabby promised.

"All right. Be careful," Greg added, closing the front door.

She called the cats, and they followed her upstairs. While they inhaled their food, Tabby crawled into the shower trying to wash away some of the exhaustion. She stood under the stream of hot water, thinking. What was she missing? What was the clue that was not clicking in her brain? She prided herself on being able to solve the mysteries on television before the end of the show. But now in real life, she was failing miserably.

Showered and dressed, she made a fresh pot of coffee. Tabby placed a call to the hardware store to verify that she had an appointment to fix the window. She relaxed in the recliner, sipping her coffee, watching the kittens play hide-and-seek with each other. As she watched them play, Tabby knew she had to go back to the drive-in. After she was done talking to Jen, she would go there and finish looking around.

Luke arrived at one-fifteen to install the new window and was done in thirty minutes. She called the alarm company, and they promised to send someone before five o'clock. The same guy who installed the original system showed up at four-thirty. The entire afternoon was wasted. Tabby didn't get to the bookstore or the drive-in as she had hoped. She decided on a light supper of just a salad and then fell into bed exhausted.

Waking up the next morning, refreshed and ready to go, Tabby put in six more hours in her shop. The inventory was set up, and the shop shelves were full. Gift baskets lined the walls closest to the front door. Six hundred jars of jelly were displayed on the shelves closest to the register. Blown-up pictures of her bridal bouquets and wedding arrangements lined the back wall of the shop. She was so excited to finally be ahead of schedule for her grand opening.

Over the next week, she would cook more batches of jelly so that she had some semblance of backstock. Closer to the opening, she would bake her gram's homemade biscuits so they would be fresh. Feeling accomplished, she decided to visit Jen at the bookstore to see what they wanted for supper. Tonight was the night for speed reading through all the compositions and deciding the winners.

"Hi, stranger," Jen said, smiling, looking up from her computer.

"Hi, yourself," Tabby commented. "What's new, beside some famous author gracing your store with her presence?"

"Pretty cool, huh?"

"Yeah, who is it and why are they in Whipper Will Junction?"

"Her name is Tricia Gracious. She's a best-selling author who's vacationing here. You know the old Gregson house on the road to Fuller's Point? Tricia bought it and is going to restore it. She agreed to do a signing, here in the shop, on Saturday morning during the Summer Kick-Off Weekend. I met with her last night and finalized all the details. She is bringing me some of her books so I can make a display in the front window telling people she will be here."

"I hope she draws a ton of customers into your shop!" Tabby exclaimed, giving her best friend a hug. "This will be the first summer festivity I am not looking forward to."

"Why not?"

"It's almost Friday, and I am no closer to finding Mr. Wells than I was the day he disappeared. I admit, the shop has preoccupied my time, and I haven't done as much as I should have done to find him," Tabby lamented.

"The sheriff hasn't had much luck either. They formed search parties and covered the woods around his house and have called in the surrounding towns to help look for him in their jurisdictions. He could be anywhere, you don't know."

"He's always been a big part of Summer Kick-Off."

"I know. He always gives the opening speech at the gazebo."

"What am I going to do, Jen? I know the answer is buried somewhere in my head, and I just can't get it to surface."

"I have been playing the conversation over and over in my head since you recited it to me. Nothing stands out except for one thing."

"What is that?" Tabby inquired.

"Fink said the demolition will wipe out all traces of evidence. Why didn't he say when the evidence was destroyed on Friday? Why demolition?"

"Oh, Jen, I could kiss you. That's what I kept passing over in my mind. I have to run," Tabby spouted excitedly.

"Glad I could help," Jen yelled, going back to her work on the computer. "Be careful."

Tabby ran all the way to the town hall. The town clerk came out of the back stacks with a large pile of papers in her hands.

"Bertha," Tabby hissed, trying to catch her breath. "Have any demolition permits been issued in Whipper Will Junction in the last month or so?"

"Just one," the pear-shaped woman answered, looking over her glasses at Tabby.

"Where? Where was it issued for?"

"The Whipper Will Drive-In is being torn down to make way for condos. I couldn't believe it myself, but they had all the right paperwork for the permit. I didn't even know it had been sold."

"Bless you, Bertha. You are a life-saver," Tabby stated as she ran out of the office.

She ran to her car as quickly as she could. She knew exactly where Mr. Wells was being held captive—the drive-in! If she had only gone back earlier like she planned, he would have been home already. Tabby reached for her cell phone only to discover that it was not in her back pocket. It was still in the kitchen on the charger. She planned on going home to start supper after her visit with Jen, but now there was no time to go back for it.

While driving like a mad woman, Tabby formed a plan in her mind. She would check out each building until she found her elderly friend. There were five buildings on the property. The projection booth was the farthest away from the entrance to the property. She would start her hunt there.

The place was deserted. There was a notice posted at the entrance warning people to stay off the property because of the upcoming demolition. She climbed out of her car and moved the saw horses to one side. Tabby drove to the back of the snack bar building where her car couldn't be seen from the entrance. As she knocked on the door, she could hear a faint groan coming from inside. She turned the knob, and the door opened easily for her.

Across the room, Mr. Wells was strapped to a cot. Under him was the duffle bag containing the stolen money. He looked at Tabby, tears forming in his eyes. She ran to him and knelt down next to the cot.

"I knew you would find me," he whispered in a hoarse voice.

"I'll get you out of here," Tabby assured him, undoing the straps that held the old man down. "We need to get you to the hospital. Crap, I wish I had my phone with me."

Mr. Wells eyes grew round in horror as he stared past Tabby. Before she could turn around, she felt a sharp pain on the back of her head, and everything went fuzzy. Her friend's eyes were the last thing she saw.

Tabby regained consciousness an hour later, her head throbbing. She looked around the room for her attacker, but no one else was there. Mr. Wells had been strapped down again on the cot and was fast asleep. Tabby assumed he had been drugged. She realized that she was cow-tied, her hands and her feet together and no matter how hard she struggled she could not seem to loosen any of the knots. They were tight and cutting into her wrists. Her feet had no feeling left in them.

It was almost dusk, and Tabby realized that soon they would be thrust into total darkness. She looked under the cot her elderly friend was laying on. The duffle bag with the money in it was gone. Her only saving grace was that her friends would be showing up at her place for dinner and she wouldn't be there. They would know that something was wrong and come looking for her. She closed her eyes trying to will away the pain in her head. Tabby knew she had to try and stay awake because the blow to her head had probably resulted in a concussion. As hard as she tried, she couldn't stay awake when the booth went dark.

GREG ARRIVED at Tabby's apartment at six-thirty. Jen and Alex arrived fifteen minutes later. Her place was in darkness.

"I don't like the look of this. I think something has happened to Tabby," Greg surmised.

"I have a key and know the alarm code. I hope she's not up there hurt," Jen lamented, leading the way up the back stairs.

She opened the door, shut off the alarm, and turned on the lights. The kittens met Jen at the door meowing loudly for their dinner.

"Tabby, are you here?" Jen yelled.

Greg pushed past her and searched the bedrooms.

"She's not here," Greg confirmed.

"Where could she be? She knew we would all be here tonight," Alex questioned.

"I told her to be careful," Jen complained. "She didn't listen to me, once again."

"What are you talking about?" Greg asked.

"We were talking about the conversation she overheard when she was listening to Fink. I said the only thing that didn't make sense to me was how he used the word demolition instead of destroy when he was talking about the evidence. She got this funny look on her face, thanked me, and ran up the street."

"Did she say where she was going?"

"No, she just ran out the door," Jen stated.

"Try to call her," Alex suggested.

"It won't do any good. Her phone is on the kitchen counter charging," Jen stated.

"You said she reacted to you talking about demolition?"

"Yes. I think she figured out where Mr. Wells was being kept."

"We need to call the sheriff and get him over here," Greg insisted, taking out his cell phone.

Minutes later, two cruisers pulled up in front of Tabby's place. The sheriff, followed by his two deputies came up the back stairs.

"Where is Tabby?" the sheriff demanded.

"We don't know. She was supposed to be cooking dinner tonight and when we arrived the place was in darkness," Greg answered, the worry showing on his face. "Jen seems to think she knew where Mr. Wells was being kept and went to get him."

"What? Are you kidding me? Doesn't that girl listen to anything anyone says?" he said, miffed. "Jen, think about the exact words you used when Tabby left."

"We were discussing the conversation she overheard at the gazebo. I told her I didn't understand why Fink used the word demolition. He could have said destroyed when he was talking about the evidence. She got all excited and ran out the door."

"Demolition set her off?"

"Yes. She ran up through the center of town, but I don't know where she went after that. She had to have come back to get her car because it's not over there where she parks it."

"Clyde, do you know anything that is set to be demolished in Whipper Will?" the sheriff queried.

"Nothing that I know of," Clyde replied.

"Me, neither," Billy said.

"Sheriff, wouldn't the town clerk know of any permits pulled for a demolition job? I bet that's where Tabby went," Greg stated.

"Let me call Bertha at home and see if Tabby visited her at the office," the sheriff said, walking away from the group to make the call.

He was only on the cell for a few minutes when he walked back to the group, frowning.

"Bertha is in Larsen, at the movies with her sister. Charlie can't get hold of her right now. He promised to have her call me immediately when she got home."

"All we can do is wait for the call from Bertha," Greg said, pacing. "Sheriff, don't you have a key to town hall?"

"I do, but it wouldn't help us. Everything is on computer now, and I don't know any of the passwords. Bertha is the only one with that information."

"What if something happened to Bertha? No one else knows the passwords?" Alex asked in astonishment.

"You have a point there. I'll have to ask her for future reference," Sheriff Puckett replied. "Right now, we have to sit tight and wait."

TABBY WOKE up to total darkness surrounding her. She had no idea what time it was or how long she had been there. Mr. Wells was groaning and rambling incoherently from the cot. She had to go to the bathroom, but she was going to hold it as long as she could.

The ropes that bound her hands had cut off her circulation. They were completely numb. She couldn't make her fingers work to undo the knots. Tabby rolled to what she thought was the direction of the door. She rolled into a solid wall. Trying again she found the door.

She inched her torso up against the door until she was sitting up. Trying to get to a kneeling position, she fell back down on the floor. Her feet were as useless as her hands. All the moving around had made the pounding in Tabby's head almost unbearable. She lay still, closed her eyes, and prayed for sleep. Mr. Wells was still babbling from the other side of the room. Once in a while, she could hear him call out her name in a raspy voice. Tabby would answer him, but he wasn't coherent enough to understand that she was right there in the room with him.

It was a little after midnight when Greg decided to stay at Tabby's apartment. There was still no call from Bertha and Jen, and Alex had gone home. The sheriff promised to come get him the minute he got the call. He dozed off in the recliner with the kittens on top of him.

Greg's cell phone rang just as the sun was cresting over the horizon.

"Charlie fell asleep waiting for his wife to get home last night. Bertha had turned her cell phone off at the cinema and forgot to turn it on again. She went to bed not even knowing about calling us. I called at five and woke them up," the sheriff informed Greg.

"Did Tabby go see her yesterday?" he mumbled, still waking up.

"Yes, she did, I know where they are. Can you get to my office in the next few minutes?"

"I'll be right there," Greg affirmed, already out the door.

He ran up Main Street to the sheriff's office. The two deputies were already there.

"Let's go," Sheriff Puckett ordered.

"Where are we going?" Greg inquired.

"The Whipper Will Drive-In."

"I should have known that," Greg fumed, mad at himself for not figuring it out before now.

The three cruisers, lights on, sped up Main Street toward the outskirts of town. The locals already at the Tilted Coffee Cup watched the speeding cars leaving town.

It only took a few minutes to reach the drive-in. A wrecking ball, bulldozers, and other equipment were already in place to begin the demolition. A crew was standing near the first building scheduled to be brought down, drinking coffee. The sheriff's car came to a screeching halt not twenty feet from them.

"Have you checked in any of the buildings?" he yelled, getting out of his cruiser.

"No, the owners told us the place had been deserted since last summer. We didn't think we needed to," the foreman answered.

"I don't want one piece of equipment to move, understand me? Two people are being held captive in one of these buildings. Spread out and help us find them," the sheriff ordered.

Greg was already running toward the projection booth which was the most isolated building on the property. He was yelling Tabby's name as he ran. The sheriff was not far behind him. They opened the door, but something was blocking the way. Together, they pushed on the door using all their weight. They didn't realize that it was Tabby's body blocking the door. It opened enough that the sheriff could stick his head in. The first thing he noticed was the strong stench of urine. The second thing was Tabby's lifeless body in front of the door.

"Call the paramedics. Get two ambulances out here," Puckett yelled to his deputy. "Greg, stop pushing on the door."

He knelt down. Using one hand, he pushed Tabby's body far enough away that he could squeeze through the opening to get in. Tabby was still unconscious, but Richard Wells recognized the sheriff since the drugs he had been given the night before were wearing off. The restraining straps were undone, and with the sheriff's help the elderly man sat up. It was the first time he realized Tabby had been locked in there with him.

Greg was kneeling next to her checking her condition. She wasn't responding to his voice. Her hair was caked with blood from the blow to the head that she had sustained.

"Tabby, please wake up," Greg pleaded. "You promised me you wouldn't go anywhere without me..."

"I'm fine, Stan, just groggy. Please help Tabby, I think she's really hurt," Mr. Wells insisted, his fight coming back to him.

Sheriff Puckett felt for a pulse.

"It's weak. Keep talking to her, Greg, until the paramedics get here."

To Greg, it seemed like forever for the ambulances to get there. Tabby was strapped to a gurney and loaded into the ambulance. Larsen General was only ten minutes away. Greg was riding in the ambulance with Tabby. The sheriff agreed to meet them there.

Mr. Wells was a different story. He refused to get in the ambulance.

"I'm not going to any public hospital smelling like an outhouse. Stan, you take me home to shower and change and only then will I agree to go and get checked out," the old man insisted. "And, on the way home, I need you to stop at the diner and pick me up something to go. I'm starving."

Realizing that the stubborn Mr. Wells was back, the sheriff gave in to his wishes. The ambulance was sent on its way back to the station. Stan waited outside of the projection booth while Mr. Wells stripped out of his urine-soaked clothes and wrapped a blanket from the trunk of the cruiser around himself. The sheriff helped his old friend into the squad car.

On the way out of the drive-in, Sheriff Puckett informed the foreman that the demolition was to be postponed indefinitely as the area was now a crime scene. They had to go through all the buildings for any evidence that might have been left behind.

On the way to the hospital, Tabby regained consciousness. The first face she saw was Greg's when she opened her eyes. She managed a weak smile.

"I know, I should have taken you with me," Tabby admitted.

"Yes, you should have. They'll be plenty of time for lectures when you feel better," Greg promised as he reached for her hand.

"Well that's something to look forward to," Tabby mumbled, closing her eyes.

The ambulance reached the hospital and Tabby was taken into one of the exam rooms. Greg was sent to the waiting area where he called Tabby's mom to let her know where her daughter was. She said she would be there as soon as possible. Twenty minutes later Samantha was being escorted to her daughter's room.

An hour later, Sheriff Puckett came through the emergency room door pushing Mr. Wells in a wheelchair. The old man did not look happy.

"Mr. Wells, you look much better already," Greg offered, smiling.

"I tried to tell Stan that, but he wouldn't listen. Insisted I come here, he did. I'll be out in twenty minutes. How's my Tabby?"

"She's been in there for a while now. Her mom is with her," Greg noted. "She was awake and talking on the ride over here. I think she just needs some rest and she'll be okay."

"Dang, fool girl," the sheriff muttered. "One of these times she'll listen to me."

"Sheriff, between you and me, Tabby is not the type of person to listen to anyone. All she knew is that her friend was in trouble and she was gone. She's been worried sick about you, Mr. Wells."

"Tabby and Jen figured out where you were, Richard. We might not have found you in time if it hadn't been for those two girls. Enough talk. Let's get you checked out so you can go home. Calypso has been well taken care of, but she has missed her owner."

"What are you waiting for then? The quicker I can get out of this dang chair, the better. Greg, please tell Tabby I will see her over the weekend."

"I will. Are you going to be well enough to make your regular speech tomorrow morning at the opening of Summer Kick-Off Weekend?"

"Don't you worry. I'll be there. Wouldn't miss it for the world. Let's go, Stan. Can't waste time sitting in no hospital. I have lots to do."

The sheriff rolled his eyes and pushed the old man to the check-in desk. They were expected and shown in immediately through the double doors. Greg could hear Mr. Wells yelling at the doctor as the doors closed.

His stomach rumbled so Greg bought a cup of coffee from the vending machine. In all the excitement, he hadn't had anything to eat or drink all morning, so even the vending machine coffee tasted good. The lady behind the desk finally called his name.

"Mr. Stone?" He nodded. "The patient in room fourteen of the green emergency wing is asking for you. Go down this hall and take your next two lefts. You'll see the room straight ahead."

Tabby was sitting up in bed when Greg entered the curtained-off room. The doctor was talking to her and looking frustrated.

"I really think you should stay overnight for observation," he insisted.

"I feel fine. I'm sore, but that will pass. I have to get home to read the compositions for tomorrow's celebration," Tabby insisted. "I promise, I'll take it easy. I'll sit in the recliner and just read."

"I think you should listen to the doctor," her mom insisted.

"Jen and Alex took the papers home with them last night and read the stories. They already have all the ribbons assigned. We didn't know if we would find you in time, so Jen took it upon herself to do it," Greg confessed.

"Now, will you stay?" the doctor asked.

"I feel fine. A few pills for this headache and I'll be good. I really don't want to stay here tonight. I would sleep much better in my own bed. Can I please have the release papers?"

"I can see I am not going to change your mind. Are you her husband?" the doctor inquired, turning to Greg.

"Not yet," Greg answered, smiling.

Samantha snickered as Tabby turned beet red.

"Oh, I'm sorry. I just assumed you were her husband. Will you be staying with her tonight? I would like someone to be there if she shows any signs of relapsing. She can only take non-aspirin medicine for that headache. If she gets worse, bring her back immediately."

"I'm not going to leave her side," Greg assured the doctor.

"Does that mean I can go home?" Tabby asked excitedly.

"Yes, I will release you, but only because you have someone staying with you tonight," he answered. "The nurse will be in shortly with the release papers."

Greg gently helped Tabby into her mom's car, and they drove in silence to her apartment. The kittens greeted their owner at the door with their normal cat-dance, followed her to the couch and crawled up to lay with her. Samantha made sure Tabby was settled in and then left to reopen her shop.

Greg made Tabby a light lunch. After she ate, she decided to rest and maybe watch a little television. He excused himself and stepped into the kitchen to call the flower shop to make sure there were no emergencies that needed his attention right away. His employees reassured him that everything was under control and they could always call him if they had any questions. Greg sat down in the recliner, relieved, and watched Tabby as she dozed in and out. The kittens were snuggled up next to her happy to have their mistress home with them.

Greg had just dozed off himself when Tabby let out a scream

"I know who the woman is!" Tabby proclaimed, sitting up. "Call the sheriff."

13

"Call the sheriff. I need to get into Fink's office to be sure," Tabby stated, throwing the blanket aside and standing up. "I don't want her to get away."

Greg called Sheriff Puckett and asked him to meet them in front of Fink's realty office with the building keys. They met on the sidewalk minutes later.

"Aren't you supposed to be resting?" Puckett inquired.

"Yes, but if I'm right, I will also be able to tell you who the dead woman was in my cellar," Tabby promised as she headed for Fink's private office.

She walked behind the desk to the small table under the window where the family pictures were displayed.

"I knew it. I told my mother that something about Lisa Carver was familiar, but I couldn't place what it was up until now. Here, look at this," Tabby said, handing the picture to the sheriff.

"It looks like Fink has a twin sister," the sheriff observed.

"The body in my cellar is the real Lisa Carver. I would stake my shop on it. Fink's sister must have killed her and applied for the position using Lisa Carver's name. Fink said she always had the desk job and was in the background while he was the front man."

"When did you see this picture?" Greg quizzed.

"The day I came in here pretending to ask about the shop rental. Fink wasn't here, and his secretary went downstairs to look for some paperwork. I nosed around while she was gone. Subconsciously, I must have seen the photo, and it stuck with me."

"I need to call the Larsen police. They need to stake out Rose Point Realty in case she returns there," the sheriff stated.

"She is probably there cleaning out all the paperwork she needs to take with her. In her mind, we are dead, so she doesn't have to hurry. There is no one left to identify her, or so she thinks," Tabby confirmed.

"Can we get you back to bed now?" Greg pleaded. "I'm sure the sheriff will call you with any updates."

"I promise," he said as he locked up the building.

Greg got Tabby settled in on the couch. He sat in the recliner, staring out the window.

"What are you thinking about?" Tabby asked.

"I was just wondering if life is always going to be this exciting with you," Greg pondered.

"We'll have to wait and see, won't we?" Tabby teased, drifting off.

Greg turned to say something, but Tabby was already asleep.

Maybe, Greg old boy, you have won her heart, and you didn't realize it.

They both slept late into the afternoon. Greg's cell phone rang, waking them up. The sheriff wanted to let them know that Fink's sister had returned to Rose Point Realty. The police were waiting for her and surprised her as she stepped through the front door. The duffle bag of money was found in the trunk of her car. The body in Tabby's shop was the real Lisa Carver.

"I guess that cleans up just about everything," Greg stated. "Want to go to the diner for supper?"

"There are still some questions I have, but only Mr. Wells can answer them for me. I'll talk to him tomorrow at the festival. And yes, I would love to go to the diner with you."

The happy couple ate dinner and returned to Tabby's apartment. Tabby had cleared out the jelly stock from the second bedroom once she had taken possession of the shop downstairs. She had purchased a new double bed so she could use it as a guest room. She just had no idea at the time that Greg would be the first one to stay in it.

"You almost got out of being my girlfriend the hard way. Don't ever take a crazy chance like that again," Greg admonished, sitting down on the edge of her bed. "I don't know what I would have done if I had gone in and found you dead."

"You didn't, so let's try to forget about it, okay?" Tabby insisted, taking Greg's hand.

"The sight of you lying there covered in blood is going to be a hard thing to forget."

"Thank you for being there," Tabby whispered quietly.

"Every day for the rest of your life," he said, bending down, kissing her tenderly on the lips. "Get some sleep. I'll be right in the next room."

Greg laid down in the second bedroom. The doors were left open, so he could hear Tabby if she needed anything. The two kittens ran back and forth between the two rooms.

"Mr. Stone?"

"What is it?"

"You do realize we are creating quite a hometown scandal," Tabby claimed. "We'll be the talk of the town tomorrow when you walk out of here in the morning."

"Do you really care?" Greg asked.

"Not in the least. Goodnight."

"Goodnight, Miss Moon."

Tabby climbed out of bed in the morning to the smells of coffee and bacon. Her first few steps were slow. She ached all over from the beating she had taken and then sleeping on the concrete floor of the projection room. She decided to take a hot shower to warm up the muscles and wash away the last of the incident. Greg had already showered and was on his second cup of coffee. Breakfast was waiting for Tabby on the table.

"A girl could get used to this," Tabby said, smiling, pouring a mug of coffee.

"I'm used to driving from Larsen. I'm up every day at five, no matter what time I go to bed."

"I guess starting next weekend, I'll be on a schedule, too," Tabby commented, walking to the front window in her living room.

The streets were filling up with people. It was only eight in the morning, but the town was already hopping. Every shop on Main Street was hosting its own event to welcome summer. Tabby's shop was the only one closed. She placed a large sign in the front window announcing the grand opening the following weekend. She didn't want her first day open being lost in the shuffle of so many activities.

The Smells So Fine Flower Shop was going to open at noon. Greg wanted to enjoy some time with Tabby before he had to attend to his own shop activities. Tabby would be spending part of the day there, sitting next to the frog fountain, making corsages for the ladies who came to visit.

The couple finished eating breakfast. Tabby set the alarm on her apartment, and they walked down the back stairs. Hiding in the alley, spying on the young couple were Mrs. Twittle and Mrs. Ryan.

"I told you that was his car," Mrs. Twittle whispered to her friend.

"He stayed overnight. Imagine that. They're not even married," Mrs. Ryan said indignantly.

"How do you know we're not married?" Greg asked with a snicker.

"I'm not falling for that again," Mrs. Twittle said, scowling.

The two women marched off toward the antique shop. They could hear Greg's laughter behind them.

"I told you we would be the talk of the town," Tabby replied, laughing. "Did you see her face? She was so mad."

It was almost nine o'clock, and Mr. Wells would be making his annual welcoming speech at the gazebo on the town green. The couple strolled over to the green, hand in hand. Their elderly friend was already up on the gazebo ready to start his speech. He tapped on the microphone to make sure he could be heard.

"Welcome, friends! It's so good to see so many of you out and about on this fine day. I won't make this long because there is so much to do around town, and I'm sure you don't want to be standing here listening to an old man babble."

There were cheers and hand-clapping.

"Hey, my speeches aren't that bad. I want to thank all the local shop owners who participated in making this event a success. At this time, I would like to add my personal thanks to Tabby Moon and Jen Jones, who without their smart thinking and quick actions, I might not be here making my annual speech. Lastly, let's give the Summer Kick-Off Weekend Committee a round of applause for the great job they have done organizing this event. Have fun, everyone, and enjoy the day."

Mr. Wells walked off the gazebo to a round of applause. He stopped in front of Greg and Tabby who had been joined by Jen and Alex. He gave Tabby and Jen a hug. He shook Greg's hand and was introduced to Alex.

"You have to tell me something, Mr. Wells. Why were you such a threat to Fink's plan?" Tabby inquired. "And what was in the safety deposit box that was so important to them?"

"I was one of the witnesses to the original will that the Swansons drew up. There was never any new will to negate the first one. I had one of the originals in my safety deposit box. The drive-in was left to Marsha's brother, Samuel Waters. I knew it and had the will prove it. The sheriff returned the key so I can give the original will to Samuel to fight the sale of the property in court. And their name wasn't Fink."

"I didn't figure it was. Who were they?" Greg interjected.

"Their real name is Carpenter. Andrew and Lily Carpenter. Lily worked in the attorney's office where the original will was drawn up. I recognized her in the wig when I went to talk to Lisa Carver about taking over my rentals. I didn't say anything, but she must have seen my facial expression when I realized who she was."

"Why was Mr. Pierce killed?" Tabby inquired.

"If that was his real name," Greg added.

"I hired him. He was a private detective that I put in the shop across the street to keep an eye on Fink. My guess is he got too close to what was happening. They must have killed him to get the recordings he made of the two of them talking in the realty office. His real name was Patrick Johnston."

"Well that answers all my questions—except one," Tabby announced.

"Why didn't you tell the sheriff who the fake Lisa Carver was when we found you?"

"When Stan brought me to the hospital the doctor said I was dehydrated. He insisted I stay until I had something to eat and an intravenous. This old body is not what it used to be, and I fell asleep for most of the afternoon. Stan came to pick me up in the early evening. He drove me home, and while we were in the car, he told me that they had arrested Lily Carpenter and recovered all the money she and her brother had stolen. You simply beat me to it!"

Mr. Wells reached into his coat pocket and brought out two envelopes. He handed one to Tabby and one to Jen.

"What is this?" Jen asked.

"This is my way of thanking you girls for saving my life. Don't open them now. Wait until you get home tonight in the privacy of your own home," the elderly man insisted. "Now, I have to go. I'm presiding over the watermelon seed spitting contest. Sheriff Puckett has won the last two years. Why don't you kids enter and try to beat him?"

"Sounds like a challenge to me," Alex replied. "Are you up for some spitting?"

"Not me. Gross. I'll watch," Jen frowned, making a face.

"I'm in," Greg agreed. "How about you, Miss Moon?"

"I'm in. Let's go."

The rest of the morning was spent walking around the town participating in many of the scheduled activities. Tabby made over thirty corsages in the two hours she was at the flower shop. Greg closed the shop at five and Tabby packed a picnic lunch for the four friends. They sat on the gazebo green, ate supper, and watched the fireworks with most of the town. At ten o'clock, the friends said good night and parted ways.

Greg stayed at Tabby's for the night instead of driving all the way back to Larsen. Sunday was his only day off, and they planned on using their leisure time to go swimming at Fuller's Point.

They sat on the couch together drinking a wine cooler.

"So, what's in the envelope?"

"I forgot all about it," Tabby said, getting up to get her purse.

She opened the envelope. Reading quietly, she suddenly gasped. A second piece of paper was stapled to the back of the letter.

"Is everything okay?" Greg wondered.

"I don't believe this," Tabby answered in amazement, setting the papers down in her lap. "This is a copy of the deed to this building. Mr. Wells is giving it to me as a thank-you for saving his life. He also gave Jen her building for figuring out the demolition angle."

"That's some gift. Are you going to accept it?" Greg asked.

"I don't know. I'll have to talk to Mr. Wells about it before I make up my mind," Tabby answered hesitantly. "But for now, I just want to get some sleep."

"If it's okay, I'm going to sit here for a while," Greg said.

"That's fine. The television remote is in the side pocket of the recliner," Tabby informed him, bending down and giving Greg a kiss.

It had been the first time that Tabby had been the one was to initiate the kiss. Greg was pleasantly surprised but kept his comments to himself.

"I'll see you in the morning, Mr. Stone."

"Yes, you will, Miss Moon."

14

Time flew by. Tabby had so many last-minute things to do for her grand opening she spent very little time with Greg. Friday night was upon her before she knew it. The next day she would be one of Whipper Will Junction's newest business owners.

She decided to hire Janice Spenser, a girl she had graduated from college with, to be her assistant in the store. It would be a full-time job until January, and then, in the winter, it would change to part-time hours. Janice agreed with that arrangement as she was a budding author who wanted to be free to write during the winter months. It worked out well for both of them.

Greg dropped by the shop and brought Tabby and Janice some dinner from the diner. They sat at the wedding table and ate. Both women had been so busy neither one realized they had worked through the supper hour.

"I have a big surprise for you tomorrow," Greg teased.

"And what would that be?" Tabby asked with lifted eyebrows.

"I'm not telling you. How would it be a surprise then?"

"He's got you there, Tabs," Janice agreed. "Thanks for supper, Greg. I'm going to run. It's going to be a long and busy day tomorrow. I need my beauty sleep."

"I am so not touching that comment," Tabby said, smiling. "I'll see you in the morning."

Ghost nimbly jumped up on the table and began nosing around the food.

"Bad kitty," Tabby scolded, as she lifted him off the table and onto the floor. "You must be hungry. It's way past your supper time."

"They seem to like the cat door I installed," Greg mentioned.

"Ghost has been up and down all day. Marmalade is still afraid of the flap."

"Are you almost done for the night?" Greg asked.

"I'm done here, but not upstairs. I have to bake at least a dozen batches of Gram's biscuits for the morning. I'm putting jelly on them and giving away samples to entice people to buy the jars."

"Great idea. Are you selling the biscuits, too?"

"Once I get going I will. Tomorrow, they are for sampling only. Want to come up and keep me company while I bake?"

"I'm sorry, I can't because I have two special orders I have to finish up tonight. Margaret couldn't take care of them, but I will be here first thing in the morning, I promise."

Tabby baked well into the night. She crawled into bed at one-thirty realizing that six-thirty was going to come very early. Even though she was exhausted, she couldn't fall asleep. The excitement of opening her own shop in less than twenty-four hours prevented her brain from slowing down enough to doze off. The last time she remembered looking at the clock, it was a little after four. She was awake and up before the alarm went off.

At seven o'clock, Tabby walked into her shop. She carried the first batch of biscuits on a silver platter and set them on the sample table. They had been cut into small pieces, and each piece would hold a small amount of jelly for tasting. She looked at the shop around her. If you were a customer walking through the front door, the first thing you saw was the wall of jelly jars. Tabby had managed to stockpile over nine hundred jars of jelly for the grand opening.

She had set up a round table with a floor-length periwinkle blue

Jellies, Jams, and Bodies

skirt by the register to highlight the jelly of the month. Blue Sin, a jelly that tasted like a blueberry pie minus the crust was the featured jelly.

The wedding corner had fresh bridal bouquets scattered around the area and a bride and groom arrangement on the consultation table. Toasting glasses, ring pillows, and other accessories needed for a wedding lined the walls.

Wedding gift baskets and jelly gift baskets filled the wall just inside the front door. A white lace curtain hung behind the register hiding the workspace out back. The sheriff had returned Jelly Bear to Tabby, and he now sat proudly on the register ready to greet people as they paid for their purchases.

An eight-foot-long table had been set up to the right of the door. Every type of jelly that Tabby offered for sale was on the sample table. Small white spoons were in a basket for people to use once and throw away. A large punch bowl was set on one end of the table. Tabby had borrowed the biggest one the lodge had for this special day. The punch was chilling. The only thing left to do was bring down the sealed containers of cut biscuits to put behind the sample table.

"Hello," Janice called from the back room. "I'm here."

It was seven-thirty. Tabby tore down the large sheets of paper that were blocking the front windows. Beautiful wedding displays filled the two front windows with jars of jellies scattered in and around the displays. People were already outside looking in the windows. The shop would open at eight.

The Smells So Fine Flower Shop truck pulled up in front of Tabby's shop. Greg jumped out of the truck and opened the back doors. He pulled a beautiful Hibiscus plant out of the truck. Tabby unlocked the front door, and Greg waltzed in with the gorgeous blooming plant and set it on the floor next to the register counter.

"Happy opening day," he said, with a swift kiss to her lips.

"It's beautiful!" Tabby exclaimed. "Thank you so much."

"Oh, it's not from me. There are ten more arrangements coming in from the different business owners in town. Do you have another table you can set up next to the register counter?"

"Seriously?" she questioned in astonishment. "Let me run upstairs for the spare table. I'll be right back."

Tabby hustled down the stairs with the table and set it up. Greg brought in each gift to the new shop owner, and they set them where everyone could enjoy them. Tabby couldn't believe how the townspeople were supporting her venture.

"Would you mind moving that big wedding gift basket on the end of the register counter?" Greg requested.

"There is still room on the table," Tabby answered.

"My gift is coming in next, and it needs a permanent place to stay. That spot would be perfect for it," Greg insisted.

"I guess I can put it on the floor in front of the basket wall," Tabby consented.

"You need to sit at the wedding table and close your eyes until I say to open them. NO peeking," Greg instructed. "Janice, would you stand in front of her so she doesn't cheat?"

Tabby sat down, and Janice made her face the far wall. Greg brought in his gift. It was a smaller version of the frog fountain that Tabby had originally fallen in love with that she had lost at the auction to Greg. It was exactly like the big one in Greg's shop. He filled it with a gallon of spring water and plugged it in. The water gurgled after a few seconds and flowed down around the frogs into the smaller lily pond. Greg walked over and placed his hand over Tabby's eyes. He led her to the counter and positioned her in front of the fountain.

"Now your shop is complete," he said, uncovering her eyes.

Tabby could not believe her eyes when she saw the miniature frog fountain and started crying.

"Why are you crying? Doesn't it make you happy?" Greg asked, crushed.

"Happier than you will ever know," Tabby replied with laughter, wiping away the tears running down her cheeks. "I can't believe you did this for me."

"I would do anything for you," Greg promised, kissing her gently on the cheek. "How about you wipe away those tears and open this shop up for business? You have quite a line forming out there."

"Look who's first in line," Tabby pointed out.

Greg turned, and Gladys Twittle had her face pressed against the door.

"Are you ready, Janice? Let's open the doors to Jellies, Jams, and Weddings," Tabby announced bursting with pride.

The shop had a steady stream of customers all day. The locals came in to buy jams and jellies by the boxfuls. Tourists came in to see why the crowds were gathering. Greg came back during his lunch hour to help out wherever he was needed. The jelly flew out of the store. Two brides booked consultations with Tabby for fall weddings. The day was a tremendous success. Five o'clock arrived before the new shop owner knew it. She stayed open an extra hour, and at six o'clock she sent Janice home and closed the doors on the first day of business.

She sat down at the wedding table, exhausted. Tabby closed her eyes, and for the first time, she was able to enjoy the sounds of her fountain.

Ghost was meowing at the cat door to be let in. Tabby thought with the high volume of traffic on an opening day it was smarter to keep them upstairs. She unlocked the cat door and Ghost came pushing through the flap.

"Come on, Marmalade. Come see me," Tabby said, calling upstairs, but the cat was nowhere to be seen.

Her jelly wall had been decimated. The one saving grace for Tabby was the store was not open on Sundays. She did not have to rush to clean things up tonight. She had all day tomorrow to do it. Greg knocked on the front door.

"Well, how did it go?" he inquired, taking her in his arms.

"Look at my jelly wall. There's nothing left. People were in and out all day, and I received several orders for cases of jelly monthly. It was wonderful."

"Do you want some help cleaning up?"

"Not tonight thanks. I'm closed tomorrow, and I have all day to reset the store. Do you want to get some supper? All I have to do is close out the register and hide the cash upstairs. In all the excitement, I forgot to get night deposit bags from the bank."

"That's a lot of money to leave around. I have a safe at the store. Do you want to lock it in my safe until Monday morning when you can take it to the bank?"

"You're right. I shouldn't leave that much money just laying around even with the alarm. Can we drive to your shop and put it in the safe?"

"Sure, we can. Do you want to go to the fish fry at the lodge?" Greg asked.

"Let me feed the cats and then we can go."

Ghost followed the couple upstairs, and Marmalade was sitting at the top of the stairs waiting for Tabby. She fed the cats. The connecting door to upstairs was locked, and Tabby emptied the register, set the alarm, and the couple left for supper. The money was safely deposited into Greg's safe.

The fish fry was well attended by many of the locals who came up to congratulate Tabby on the opening of her shop. She was laughing and enjoying her evening with Greg when exhaustion hit her. All of a sudden, Tabby could hardly keep her eyes open. Greg noticed how quiet she had become and suggested that they head home. He parked out back next to Tabby's car.

"Are you coming up?" Tabby asked, yawning.

"No, it's twenty minutes to Larsen, and if I don't go now, I may fall asleep behind the wheel."

"You could stay here. I have the second bedroom, and it's not like you haven't been seen leaving here in the morning already," Tabby suggested.

"That would be nice, I am really tired."

"Good, lock up the car and let's go upstairs."

Greg grabbed the spare clothes he kept in his trunk. Mr. Wells had promised him the rental house in Whipper Will Junction, and soon, his ride home would take under five minutes.

Once upstairs, Tabby took a shower, and Greg followed close behind. They snuggled on the sofa for a while, and Tabby tried to stifle a yawn.

"Am I boring you?" Greg joked.

"I'm sorry, I am just so tired," Tabby apologized.

"Let's go to bed," Greg said, picking her up and carrying her to her room.

He tucked her in, called the kittens up on the bed, and turned off the lights. He started walking down the hall toward the second bedroom.

"Greg," Tabby called out from the darkness.

"Yeah," he said, walking back and sticking his head through the doorway.

"Thank you for everything, and I'm glad we shared the booth at the diner," Tabby said quietly.

"I'm glad, too. I guess I'll stick around for a while."

He shut off the lights in the hallway and retired to the spare bedroom. Marmalade stayed with Tabby while Ghost followed and slept with Greg.

This would be the first of many more mysteries to come.

THE END

RECIPE

AL'S BACKWOODS BERRIE LLC.

14 KING PHILLIPS ROAD

PLYMOUTH, MASSACHUSETTS 02360

BLUEBERRY SIN JELLY

- 2 Large Pans (one for cooking, one for sterilizing the jars)
- Wooden Spoon (for strength)
- 2 Pounds of Fresh Blueberries or equivalent of frozen berries
- 1 Package of Store-Bought Pectin 1.75 ounce
- 7 Cups of Sugar
- 8 - 8 Ounce Mason Jars with Lids
- Ground Cinnamon (to taste)

Place blueberries into a large saucepan and bring to a boil while constantly stirring. Add pectin slowly and bring back to a boil. Start to add sugar, slowly, constantly stirring to prevent the sugar from burning. Bring mixture to a hard boil for one minute.

In the larger pan, place the eight jars and covers in water, submerged completely, and bring to a boil. Remove jars, one at a time and fill with jelly. Place lid on jar, invert the full jar for thirty seconds to seal, then turn upright and let cool.

This should yield 8 - 8-ounce jars of jelly.

Equivalents:

1 pint of fresh berries = ¾ pound or 2 ½ cups blueberries

1 quart of fresh berries = 1 ½ pounds or 4 cups

Printed in Great Britain
by Amazon